The
Haunted States
of America...

Haunted Houses and Spooky Places in All 50 States . . . and Canada, Too!

by Joan Holub

ALADDIN PAPERBACKS

New York   London   Toronto   Sydney   Singapore

If you purchased this book without a cover you should be aware that this book is stolen property. It was reported as "unsold and destroyed" to the publisher and neither the author nor the publisher has received any payment for this "stripped book."

First Aladdin Paperbacks edition September 2001

Aladdin Paperbacks
An imprint of Simon & Schuster
Children's Publishing Division
1230 Avenue of the Americas
New York, NY 10020

All rights reserved, including the right of reproduction in whole or in part in any form.
The text of this book was set in Stone Informal.
Designed by Sammy Yuen Jr.
Printed and bound in the United States of America.
10 9 8 7 6 5 4 3 2 1

CIP data for this book is available from the Library of Congress.

ISBN 0-689-83911-1

FOR BOO-TIFUL BARBARA, EERIE EMILY,
SPOOKY SARA, AND CHAIN-RATTLING RON
—J. H.

This book deals with a controversial subject. It contains the ideas and opinions of its author, based on gathered resource material. The theories expressed in this book are not the only possible interpretations of the covered subject matter. Readers are invited to make a judgment based on all information that is available. The information herein is sold with the understanding that the author is not engaged in rendering any professional service in the book. The author disclaims responsibility for any liability, loss, risk (including personal and other types of risk), incurred indirectly or directly as a consequence of reading this book.

Are Ghosts Real?

Do you believe in ghosts?

Many people claim they have seen ghosts or visited places haunted by them. The very mention of "ghosts" has caused emperors, kings, and company presidents alike to shake in their shoes. Shakespeare included ghosts in many of his plays. Early Romans told ghost stories. Ancient Egyptians mummified their dead so that their spirits would have pleasing forms to inhabit. Even Stone Age people drew pictures of spirits on their cave walls.

If ghosts are real, why are so many hanging around? People who died tragically or unexpectedly seem the most likely to return as spirits after death. Do they long for something or someone they left behind? Do they roam the earth because they have unfinished business here? Are they hoping to right a wrong, get revenge, or deliver a warning? Are they trying to scare us? Or are they just curious or lonely? Who knows?

Only one thing is for sure: Houses, schools,

libraries, caves, hotels, ships, and other places rumored to be haunted can be found all over the United States, Canada, and around the world. Ghostly images, weird knocks, eerie laughter, strange lights, and unexplained whispers have been reported at many of these sites.

Are you ready to be scared silly? Are you brave enough to venture inside not just one—but fifty-five places that might be haunted? Then step into a world where every day is unlucky Friday the 13th and every night is Halloween. And read on, IF YOU DARE. . . .

Alabama
Railroad Bill: the Robin Hood of Alabama?

Location: Limestone County, Alabama

Some people say Railroad Bill was a sort of Robin Hood, who stole from the Louisville and Nashville Railroad (L&N) and gave to the poor people of Alabama. Others think he was just a rotten outlaw.

Beginning in October 1859, the Louisville and Nashville Railroad ran passenger and freight trains along a track system 187 miles long. Its route stretched from Louisville, Kentucky, to Nashville, Tennessee. The L&N thrived during the period of rebuilding after the Civil War. By 1872, it went all the way to Alabama, where it ran through Birmingham and Montgomery, and later to Mobile. But the poorest residents of Alabama could barely afford food, much less a railroad ticket.

According to legend, Railroad Bill stole food and whatever else he could from the railroad's freight trains. But he didn't eat all of the tasty loot himself. He shared it with Alabama's poor, often leaving it on their shack porches as a gift.

Even if he did have a generous side, Bill was undoubtedly a lawless hooligan. He carried a rifle and two guns and wasn't shy about using them. Beginning in 1894, he had run-ins with police and railroad workers. A year later, he shot and killed an Alabama sheriff. A reward was offered for his arrest.

Somehow Bill always managed to evade capture. He escaped the law so easily and often that people began to wonder if he was indestructible. Some said mere gunshots couldn't kill him. Others said he could catch bullets with his bare hands. It was even whispered that he could transform himself into a dog to blend in with the sheriffs' bloodhounds.

Eventually, Railroad Bill proved himself to be mortal. He was killed by a constable in Atmore, Alabama, on March 7, 1897.

By the end of 1971, the Louisville and Nashville Railroad operated over 6,500 miles of track through thirteen states. The railroad eventually became part of a company called CSX Transportation. But thousands of miles of L&N track still exist and are in use today.

Over the past century, the ghost of Railroad Bill has been reported wandering along Alabama railroad tracks and in nearby pinewoods. He is described as a thirty-eight-year-old, wide-shouldered African-American man, known for his broad smile.

From time to time, poor Alabama residents still find donations of food on their porches. Are the gifts from the ghost of Railroad Bill? Some people think so.

Alaska
Gold Rush Ghosts

Location: Skagway, Alaska

If you believe the rumors, the town of Skagway is full of ghosts.

In 1896, prospectors struck gold in the Klondike region of Canada's Yukon Territory. The discovery was close to the Canadian border near the Alaskan town of Skagway. When news of the strike spread, a gold rush began. Skagway became known as "the gateway to the gold rush" and grew into a boomtown with an amazing population of 20,000.

Miners hoping to strike it rich left Seattle, Washington, and traveled to Skagway by ship. From there, they went farther north along the difficult trails to Canada's gold country. The treacherous trip ended the lives of many prospectors. Avalanches buried some of them. Some slid on ice in mountain passes and fell to their deaths in the valleys below. Still others became deathly ill from the bone-chilling cold.

Skagway is the only Alaska boomtown that didn't eventually burn down or become deserted. Many of the original buildings still stand today, and ghosts from the gold rush days reportedly lurk around.

Some people say there's a ghostly guest inhabiting room 24 of the oldest hotel in Alaska, the three-story gold-domed Golden North. Dressed in a white wedding gown, the ghost of a woman has been peering from a window awaiting the return of her fiancé for a hundred years. Unfortunately, he's not coming back. He died in 1890s, on the difficult trek north to hunt for gold. Too frightened to venture out into the wild streets of boomtown Skagway, the young woman hid in room 24. She eventually died of pneumonia.

Most hotel visitors never see the ghost of room 24. But some *do*. One couple even claimed that a ghost climbed into their bed! Other guests complained that someone walked in and out of the room during the night. Construction workers staying in room 24 once fled the hotel in the middle of the night with no explanation. Had they been scared away by a ghost in a wedding gown?

The Red Onion Saloon in Skagway is also rumored to be haunted. The downstairs portion is still a saloon. Upstairs areas are used as offices, and are where most of the spooky activity reportedly occurs:

☞ A downstairs bartender was once so frightened by footsteps above her on the second floor that she called the police. When they arrived, police heard the steps, too. But when they checked, they found no one walking around upstairs.

☞   One day, an upstairs office door which didn't have a lock suddenly refused to open. A few minutes after efforts to open it were halted, the door was inexplicably found standing wide open.

☞   A musician, who played at the saloon and then slept upstairs overnight, once woke to see a strange, glowing shape in his room.

Other employees have felt sudden cold areas of air and smelled heavy perfume in the saloon, occurrences for which there was no known explanation.

Skagway's Mulvihill House is thought to be haunted by "Mul" Mulvihill, a man who lived there from 1914 to 1949. In his work as dispatcher for the White Pass and Yukon Route Railroad, Mul often used a telegraph. Some people say they hear the ghostly *tap-tap-tap* of an invisible telegraph key in his house.

These are just a few of the many buildings in Skagway that are reputedly haunted. Why would ghosts want to haunt this town? Maybe they were attracted to the tragedy and turmoil Skagway once experienced. During its get-rich-quick gold rush days many people arrived in Skagway with high hopes, only to meet terrible fates. Some unlucky newcomers were swindled out of their money. Others starved to death, were shot, or died in the diphtheria epidemic. Not to mention all of the prospectors who perished on their way to the Klondike.

Skagway is now part of the Klondike Gold Rush National Historic Park, and only about a thousand people live there. One of the town's primary industries is tourism, and some of the locals dress in fashions popular during the gold rush days. The *clip-clop* sound of horse-drawn buggies can be heard as visitors are taken on sight-seeing trips. Skagway residents wave and smile. But look more closely. You might spy some friendly ghosts among the living!

Arizona
Superstition Mountain Spooks

Location: The Superstition Mountains, east of Phoenix, Arizona

The ghosts in the Superstition Mountains are not a happy bunch. Many of them lost their lives while searching for a great gold mine known as the Lost Dutchman.

The Lost Dutchman Mine is one of the most famous treasure legends in the United States. Researchers think it was originally discovered by the Peralta family, who were later killed by Apaches. A man named Jacob Waltz is believed to have relocated the gold mine in the 1800s. The mine was nicknamed after him, though he was actually German rather than Dutch.

The location of this mine is a mystery today. No one is sure it even exists. Waltz told no one where it was before he died, but he did leave clues behind. These clues have encouraged thousands of people to hunt for the gold mine over the years. As many as one hundred have died in the effort.

Legend has it that those who search for treasure in the Superstition Mountains are doomed. Human skeletons of unknown identity have been discovered in the mountains from time to time. What happened to these men?

Apache myth tells of a Thunder God that lives in the Superstition Mountains and protects the mountains from trespassers.

In the 1800s, Native Americans killed some treasure hunters, whom they saw as troublemakers invading their land.

The deaths of others were more mysterious. In 1931, a man named Adolf Ruth may have come close to rediscovering the Lost Dutchman gold mine. He found a map, possibly created by the Peralta family, showing the mine's location. Ruth set out to find the treasure, but never made it. His headless body was found in the Superstition Mountains weeks later.

A prospector named James Kidd went into the mountains in search of treasure in 1949. He never returned.

Many think that the ghosts of Jacob Waltz and other prospectors still wander the mountains. No one is sure why. Perhaps they are jealously guarding their treasure. Or maybe they believe the treasure is cursed and are trying to warn others against searching for it—before they wind up as ghosts, too!

Arkansas
Ghosts of the Crescent Hotel

Location: Eureka Springs, Arkansas

If you like ghosts, you might want to stay in room 218 at the Crescent Hotel. Imagine waking up in the middle of the night in a strange hotel room to find a ghost staring at you. At least one visitor staying in the room said this happened to him!

Another guest was reportedly pushed out of bed in room 218 by someone or something invisible.

There is even a story that a woman staying in the room once ran screaming from it in the middle of the night. She said there was blood splashed on its walls. When the room was inspected, no blood was found. Had she been dreaming—or did something strange really happen that night?

A hotel employee once tried to show this room to guests, but encountered an odd problem. When he tried to push the door open, someone pushed back from inside the room. After a brief struggle, he finally got the door open. There was no one inside.

Is there really a pesky ghost haunting room 218? If so, who is it?

The Crescent Hotel was built as a vacation resort around 1885. During the hotel's construction, a Swedish workman named Michael is said to have fallen to his death in the area where room 218 is now. His description matches that of the ghost people have seen: muscular, blond, blue-eyed, wearing clothing typical of a carpenter or stonemason.

Michael is a goofy ghost, who seem to enjoy playing tricks on hotel maids. He tugs on their carts, flips TVs and lights on and off, and bangs on walls.

Michael may not be the only spirit at the Crescent Hotel. A distinguished gentleman ghost dressed in old Victorian-style clothing has been seen more than once in the hotel lobby and bar. Ghosts have also been spotted in rooms 202 and 424, though no one knows who they might be.

The Crescent Hotel saw hard times in the early 1900s. It became a women's college for a while. Then, in 1937, a man named Norman Baker bought it and turned it into a hospital. Though he had no apparent medical training, Baker began developing and selling medicines. He even peddled a "cure" for cancer. Most of his cures were dismissed as quackery, and authorities eventually imprisoned him for fraud. Some believe Baker's ghost lurks on the hotel's first-floor stairs.

Today, the lovely Crescent Hotel is still popular with guests—and possibly with ghosts as well.

California
Winchester Mystery House

Location: San Jose, California

What has 160 rooms, secret passageways, dead-end stairs, doors to nowhere, and took thirty-eight years to build? The Winchester Mystery House in San Jose, California.

Sarah Winchester believed in ghosts—both good and bad ones. Her husband, William, was the son of Oliver Winchester, the manufacturer of the famous Winchester repeating rifle. When Sarah's husband died in 1881, he left her millions of dollars earned from sales of the popular rifle. Over the years, the rifle had been used to kill thousands of people, many of them Native Americans. Sarah feared that the angry ghosts of these victims had cursed the Winchester fortune and had killed her husband. Her biggest worry was that they might get *her* next.

She decided to visit a spiritual medium in Boston, Massachusetts, for help. The medium confirmed Sarah's worst fears: The spirits *were* mad, he told her there was only one way she could escape their wrath.

14

She had to build a big house in which to hide.

Sarah was determined to do whatever it took to stay safe from evil spirits. In 1884, she purchased an eight-room farmhouse on forty-four acres of land in what is now San Jose. And she began building. Her farmhouse quickly grew in every direction until it became a sprawling Victorian mansion. Construction on the house continued night and day, seven days a week, for the next thirty-eight years of her life. Sarah believed that if building stopped for one moment, the angry spirits would attack her.

Although she desperately wanted bad spirits kept out of her house, Sarah encouraged good spirits to visit. Every night, servants rang a bell in her tower three times. The first ring was at the stroke of midnight, the others at one and two A.M. These were calls for good spirits to gather in the Blue Room, a windowless, secret room where Sarah held séances. Once she had gathered these "good" spirits together, she sought their advice regarding what to build onto her house next.

These good spirits must have had very strange ideas about architecture. Under their instruction, Sarah developed some truly odd house plans. But all of the plans had a single purpose: to keep bad spirits away. The reason the house has so many maze-like hallways, secret rooms, as well as stairs, doors, and windows leading to nowhere was that Sarah was trying to confuse the bad spirits so they could not find her. She even slept in a different bedroom each night, hoping to elude them.

Thirteen must have been Sarah Winchester's lucky number. Her house has thirteen bathrooms, the thirteenth of which has thirteen windows. There are thirteen windows *and* thirteen doors in the sewing room. The greenhouse has thirteen cupolas. Thirteen palm trees line the main driveway to the house, and the staircase has thirteen steps. In the Blue (séance) Room, there are thirteen wall hooks for the thirteen robes she often wore during séances. Sarah even signed her name thirteen times on her will!

For thirty-eight years, construction was constant at Sarah Winchester's house. But on September 5, 1922, all construction halted when she died at age eighty-three.

Some psychics and other visitors claim the Winchester Mystery House really is haunted. Sarah's gray-haired ghost has been spotted in one of the kitchens, and there have been sightings of strange floating lights in one of her bedrooms. Mysterious whispers echo, doors bang, floors creak and organ music plays when no one is in the house—at least no one living!

The Winchester Mystery House has been placed on the National Register of Historic Places. Guided tours of the house are offered to the public, with special festivities on Halloween and Friday the 13th.

Colorado
Spooky Silver Cliff Cemetery

Location: Silver Cliff, Colorado

Dozens of mysterious blue lights twinkle over tombstones in Silver Cliff Cemetery on dark, lonely nights.

Back in the 1880s, Silver Cliff was a silver-mining boomtown of nearly five thousand residents. Miners passing the town cemetery one night in 1882 were the first in recorded history to see strange lights floating among the tombstones. The miners could hardly believe their eyes, and hurried to tell everyone in town what they'd seen.

Few others believed them, since the miners had all been drunk when they'd seen the blue lights. Still, one curious group that included a lawyer, a photographer, a storekeeper, and other respectable citizens ventured to the graveyard several nights later. They wanted to see for themselves if there was any truth to the wild story. At first they saw nothing, but then lights began popping out everywhere. The drunken miners' tale *was* true!

Escaping bog or methane gases, reflections from

faraway lights, and uranium radiation have all been suggested as possible causes for the lights. However, these theories have holes in them. Escaping gases are usually visible above marshes—but there's no water in this cemetery. Gases sometimes rise above earth that contains decaying matter—but all of the bodies buried here decayed long ago. Because the lights usually appear on rainy, snowy, or foggy nights, it is unlikely they are simply reflections. Lights from nearby towns don't shine as far as the cemetery when skies are overcast. Geiger counters have been brought to the area, but little radiation was found. It has also been suggested that the lights could result from ball lightning, earthquakes, or volcanic activity.

The truth is that no one really knows for sure who or what causes the blue lights.

Some people think the lights may be the spirits of German and English settlers and miners buried long ago in the old cemetery. It's also possible that Native American tribes may have once buried their dead where the more modern cemetery now lies. Native American legend tells of "dancing blue spirits" inhabiting their burial sites.

In the 1960s, articles in *The New York Times* and *National Geographic* made the Silver Cliff Cemetery lights famous. One editor actually saw the lights during his visit to the cemetery in 1969. He described them as "dim, round spots of blue-white light." He and another man followed one of the lights for about fifteen minutes, but couldn't catch it.

The whimsical lights seem able to appear and

disappear at will. Sometimes they bob and weave above the tombstones. They may float as high as twenty feet in the air before drifting back down. Some witnesses claim to have seen seventy or more lights at once.

Through the years many have tried to solve the mystery of these dancing blue lights. But no one has managed it yet!

Connecticut
The Dudleytown Curse

Location: Dudleytown, Connecticut

These days it's DEAD quiet in Dudleytown. That is, except for the occasional disembodied murmurs and the dark spirits some people sense there. Over one hundred spooky incidents have been reported at Dudleytown, leading some ghost hunters to proclaim it one of the most haunted places in America.

In 1737, Dudleytown was settled by the Dudley brothers: Abiel, Barzillai, and Gideon. The brothers were originally from England, where some members of their family had experienced bad luck in the past. In the 1500s, two Dudleys were beheaded when they tried to overthrow the English king. Another Dudley may have accidentally brought a plague from France to England. Rumors began to circulate that the Dudley family was cursed.

When the Dudley brothers moved to Connecticut, the so-called family curse may have come with them. Insanity and other tragedies seemed to plague Dudleytown from the start. Abiel Dudley himself was reportedly among those who went insane. Abiel's neighbor lost his sanity after being suspected of murder. After one woman was killed by a lightning bolt, her husband slowly lost his mind. Yet another Dudleytown man returned from a business trip to find his wife laughing insanely. U.S. presidential candidate Horace Greeley married a woman from Dudleytown named Mary Cheney. She committed suicide in 1872.

For a settlement of a mere one hundred residents, Dudleytown certainly seemed to have more than its fair share of trouble. Few new families moved in over the years, perhaps fearing it truly was cursed. The town slowly died.

Dudleytown never had much chance of survival in the first place. It was founded in an area with a cold climate and rocky soil. Growing profitable crops was difficult, so Dudleytown farmers had turned to charcoal production. This was dangerous because work areas were often poorly ventilated. Inhaling too much charcoal dust can lead to oxygen deprivation, which could help explain any insanity in Dudleytown.

Dudleytown has been a ghost town since 1924. Many people feel uncomfortable there, sensing what could be unhappy spirits. Some visitors claim to have been nudged, pushed, or grabbed by unseen forces. One man said a branch was thrown at him when no one was around to throw it. Others find that ghostly images appear in photos taken there.

It is said that the longer you stay in Dudleytown, the more bad luck you'll have afterward. It's considered especially bad luck to take a souvenir, even one as tiny as a stone or leaf, from the town.

Nearby communities do not like talk of Dudleytown curses or ghosts. Tales of such have lured witches, Satan worshipers, treasure hunters, ghost hunters, and vandals to their area. Some of these visitors have been destructive, so it's understandable that Dudleytown's neighbors discourage more tourists from coming around. Currently, the Dudleytown area is privately owned by a group known as the Dark Entry Forest Association. Trespassing is prohibited.

Delaware
Governor's Mansion Ghosts

Location: Dover, Delaware

A hanging man, a young girl, and a 1700s dandy are all said to haunt the Delaware Governor's Mansion, also known as the Woodburn Mansion. Why would three ghosts who don't know each other haunt the same place? It seems possible that they all had some relationship to the house during their lifetimes.

The Woodburn Mansion was built in 1790, and was owned by a man named Daniel Cowgill during the Civil War. Cowgill was a Quaker, who did not believe in slavery. While he lived in the mansion, it became a busy stop along the famous slave escape route known as the Underground Railroad. Cowgill hid slaves in his cellar. He even dug a tunnel through which slaves could flee from his home toward Free States or Canada.

One night, men visited the mansion planning to capture slaves and sell them. Cowgill managed to fend them off—all except for one who hid in an old poplar tree near the house. This man probably hoped

to sneak into the cellar and kidnap slaves when Cowgill wasn't looking. However, his plan went awry. He slipped and accidentally hanged to death when his head became wedged between two branches.

Today, that two hundred-year-old poplar tree still stands outside the Woodburn Mansion. It is known as Dead Man's Tree, or the Hanging Tree, and many people find it spooky. The hanged man's ghost can supposedly be seen dangling from this tree on moon-lit nights.

In the 1940s, the ghost of a little girl wearing a red-checked dress was first reported at the mansion. She was spotted playing beside the reflecting pool in the gardens.

The Woodburn Mansion became the official home of the governor in 1966, when it was bought by the state of Delaware. During Governor Michael Castle's 1985 inauguration party at the mansion, one guest thought she saw the ghost of the small girl in a corner of the room. Others felt her tug on their clothing.

Later that year, several sixth-grade students and their teacher stayed in the mansion overnight. They were hoping to find out who the little girl might be. Though they weren't able to learn anything about the ghostly girl, something weird did happen: The paint-ing of a woman smiled at them!

A dapper gentleman ghost has also been seen in the mansion. He wears knee-length pants, a ruffled shirt, and a white powdered wig, as was fashionable for men in the 1700s. This ghost likes to have a glass of wine from time to time. Before the house became the governor's residence, people living there some-times left wine out overnight for him. By the next morning, the wine glasses were empty! Some servants even saw him drink from a wine decanter in the dining room. *Cheers!*

District of Columbia (Washington, D.C.)
White House Ghosts

Location: 1600 Pennsylvania Avenue N.W., Washington, D.C.

The White House very well may be the most haunted house in America! It is better known as the private home of the president of the United States and his or her family. Every time a new president is elected, the old president moves out of the White House and the new president moves in—at least, the old presidents are supposed to leave. Some of their ghosts may stick around instead!

President Abraham Lincoln is the most famous person who supposedly haunts the White House. Lincoln may have been something of a psychic. In 1865, he dreamed he would soon be assassinated. Just days later, he was shot and killed by John Wilkes Booth while watching a play at Ford's Theatre in Washington, D.C.

Winston Churchill, President Harry Truman, First Lady Eleanor Roosevelt, and many others have reportedly sensed Lincoln's presence. But Grace Coolidge, wife of President Calvin Coolidge, was probably the first to see Lincoln's ghost during the 1920s. She is said to have seen him standing in the Yellow Oval Room gazing out of a window located over the front entrance to the White House. Lincoln had spent a lot of time in this room during his term as president.

Some say that Lincoln's ghost haunts the Lincoln Bedroom, on the second floor of the White House as well. A maid during Franklin Roosevelt's term claimed she saw Lincoln's ghost sit on the bed and put on a pair of boots.

The most famous member of royalty to see his ghost was probably Queen Wilhelmina of the Netherlands. She was alone in the Rose Bedroom, across the hall from the Lincoln Bedroom, when she heard a knock at her door. She opened it, saw what appeared to be the ghost of Abraham Lincoln standing the hallway, and promptly fainted dead away. When she came to, he was gone.

According to the following four legends, the ghosts of other former U.S. presidents and their wives also visit the White House now and then:

☞ President William Henry Harrison's ghost hangs out in the attic, dragging furniture around.
☞ President Andrew Jackson's ghost laughs, curses, and yells in the Rose bedroom.
☞ President John Adams moved into the house around 1797, and was the first U.S. president to live there. The ghost of his wife, Abigail, hangs laundry and passes through walls in the East

Room on the ground floor. Since it was warm and dry, the East Room was the best place to hang laundry while she lived in the White House.

☞ President James Madison's wife, Dolley, was one of the most popular first ladies in history. She planted the beautiful White House Rose Garden, where press conferences are still held today. Dolley's ghost once returned to thwart President Woodrow Wilson's wife's plans to dig up the Rose Garden. After Dolley's ghost scolded the gardeners, they refused to do the work.

Are the president and his family really living in a haunted house? The White House Visitors Center conducts regular tours of the White House. So you can visit and ask the tour guides if they have seen any ghosts. You won't get to peek into the Lincoln Bedroom, though. Because the White House is the private home of the president's family, many of its rooms are off-limits to visitors—but maybe not to ghosts!

Florida
The Spooky Doll

Location: Key West, Florida

When five-year-old Robert Eugene "Gene" Otto did something wrong, he sometimes claimed he hadn't done it. This isn't so unusual—many children do the same thing to avoid punishment. However, unlike other children, Gene is reported to have blamed his misdeeds on his life-size doll. This misbehaving doll was named Robert, too. But it shared more than just a name with its young owner. It also looked like him.

Robert (the doll) was created in 1904, at a time when families commonly had life-size dolls made to look like their children. He had eyes made of buttons, and several sets of clothing. His outfits, which included a sailor suit, were copies of the very ones little Gene wore.

Gene and his doll shared an upstairs bedroom just below a turret in a two-story Victorian house in Key West. The house had been built in 1890 by Gene's grandfather, Thomas. Many artists lived in Key West, and when Gene grew up he became an artist, too. He turned the turreted room that had once been his bed-room into an art studio. Did Robert's button eyes watch him as he worked? Maybe!

In more recent years, it has been rumored that workmen at the house have seen the doll act oddly. One heard the doll giggle. Others said the doll was able to move by itself. It seemed to suddenly appear in different locations around the house—like magic.

There have also been tales of pictures flying off the walls, and of doors opening or locking on their own in Gene's turreted studio. The steps leading to the studio are said to be especially spooky. Some people have felt strange, cold gusts of wind and heard windows rattle along these stairs.

The house is now a popular bed-and-breakfast inn.

Georgia
The Waving Girl

Location: Elba Island, Georgia

From 1887 to 1931, ships sailing into the mouth of the Savannah River from the Atlantic Ocean were always greeted with a friendly wave. A woman named Florence Martus ran out of her house on Elba Island and waved to greet every ship that passed on its way into Savannah Harbor. During the day, Florence flapped her white apron in a breezy hello. At night, she swung a lantern to and fro in welcome.

Florence's brother was the lighthouse keeper on Elba Island, and she lived in a house nearby. Elba Island lies about seven miles southeast of the city of Savannah. James Oglethorpe and 125 English settlers founded Savannah in 1733. Eli Whitney invented the cotton gin near Savannah just sixty years later. Georgia's ship trade prospered as cotton became a profitable crop. Many ships began to sail past Elba Island on their way inland to Savannah. Ship captains and their crews looked forward to Florence's friendly waves.

But Florence Martus was not just being friendly: Each time she saw a ship approach, hope rose inside her. Would this be the ship carrying her beloved fiancé? He had left one day, promising to return. Florence had vowed she would greet every passing ship until he finally did. That way, when he sailed home and saw her waving, he would know she still loved him.

But Florence never saw her fiancé again. In 1931, her brother retired after forty-four years as the island's lighthouse keeper. Once his job ended, he and Florence moved away. The waving girl's vigil ended. Or did it?

Today, Savannah is a major seaport, visited by hundreds of vessels every year. In Florence Martus's memory, ships often toot their horns in greeting as they enter Savannah Harbor. Some crewmen claim her ghost waves to them, ever hopeful that her fiancé might be onboard their ship.

Located next to Savannah's busy port, River Street is a lively tourist area. It is lined with old cotton warehouses, some of which have been remodeled into shops and restaurants. In their shadow stands a bronze statue of Florence Martus. She is waving her apron and looking out to sea, with her dog by her side. The statue's plaque reads:

Florence Martus
1869–1943
Savannah's Waving Girl

Hawaii
Volcano Goddess Madame Pele

Location: Mainland Hawaii

If you ever see volcano goddess Madame Pele, you'd better look out! A volcanic eruption won't be far behind.

According to Hawaiian mythology, Pele has lived on the big island of Hawaii for over two hundred years. She makes her home deep in the bubbling hot lava of the fire pit Halemaumau, inside the Kilauea caldera. Crater-shaped Kilauea is about two and a half miles long and two miles wide. It is located on the eastern slope of another volcano, 13,677-foot-tall Mauna Loa.

Ever since the 1950s, Kilauea has periodically erupted. If Pele is seen just before such an eruption, she looks tired and elderly. When seen afterward, she looks beautiful and young.

Island dwellers do their best to keep Pele happy so she'll keep the volcanoes quiet. They leave traditional offerings such as pork, fish, berries, flowers, and bananas as gifts for her at the volcano's rim. The manager of one hotel is said to pour gin into Kilauea on a regular basis to soothe her. This seems to have worked so far. Whenever eruptions seem certain to destroy his hotel, lava mysteriously flows away from it instead.

In 1904, a group of men had an unusual encounter at a luau near Kilauea's rim. The volcano had been rumbling all day, and everyone expected flames and red-hot lava to shoot skyward at any minute. (Today, it's unlikely that anyone would be allowed so close to the volcano before an eruption. But in those days, people often took dangerous risks to get the best possible view.)

As the men feasted on roast pig, poi, and other Hawaiian delicacies, an elderly woman with long gray hair wandered by. Though they didn't know her, the men graciously invited her to share their food. She refused, saying, "I have work to do." Immediately upon uttering the words, she leaped into the crater.

The men stared in amazement. Had they just met Madame Pele? Surely only she would enjoy a swim in boiling lava. They didn't have much time to ponder the question. Minutes after the woman jumped, flames and lava burst from the crater. The men took off, escaping safely on their horses. But they never forgot that night and always wondered if they truly had met Pele.

There is another legend that says Pele curses those who steal from her. Many tourists claim they've had bad luck after removing lava rock from her crater. In fact, park rangers at Hawaii Volcanoes National Park sometimes receive mail containing lava rocks. The returned rocks come from tourists who have taken them as souvenirs and, once they've heard the rocks are jinxed, don't want them anymore.

In 1991, a Hawaiian newspaper printed a copy of a letter from a couple of such tourists. Enclosed with their letter apologizing to Madame Pele was some returned lava rock. They begged Pele's forgiveness and said they had taken her rock without realizing she wouldn't like it. Since taking the rock, they felt their luck had been bad. By returning it, they hoped their luck would change for the better.

Does Pele really have the power to cause bad luck to those who steal from her? If you ever visit Hawaii, don't swipe any lava rocks—just in case.

Idaho
Spirit Lake Sweethearts

Location: Spirit Lake, Idaho

A Native American tribe known as the Kootenai (Water People) once lived on the shores of Spirit Lake. Today, the Spirit Lake area is home to about one thousand residents—or one thousand and *two,* if you count the lake's two ghosts.

According to a legend of long ago, a beautiful Kootenay girl named Fearless Running Water and a Kootenay brave named Shining Eagle fell in love. They hoped to marry one day, but there was a problem.

Unfortunately, someone else had fallen in love with Fearless Running Water, too. His name was Yellow Serpent, and he was the chief of an enemy tribe. Yellow Serpent wanted to marry Fearless Running Water, whether she wanted to marry him or not. He threatened to attack the Kootenai if she refused. To prevent a war, Fearless Running Water's father told to wed Yellow Serpent.

Fearless Running Water and Shining Eagle were very upset. They vowed to love each other forever, no

39

matter what. One night, they made a tragic decision. They went to Suicide Cliff, wove a ceremonial marriage chain from long marsh grasses, and tied it around themselves. Together, they jumped into Spirit Lake.

The lake is four and a half miles long, one mile across, and one hundred feet deep. The bodies of the two lovers were never found. They probably either drowned or were killed from the fall.

On moonlit nights, a phantom canoe is said to glide silently through Spirit Lake. The ghosts of Fearless Running Water and Shining Eagle guide their canoe as though still searching for an escape from their situation. The haunting sound of their paddles slapping the water echoes eerily across the lake. Or is that just the wind?

Illinois
Resurrection Mary

Location: Resurrection Cemetery, in Justice, Illinois

Never pick up a hitchhiker, especially if you're driving in Justice, Illinois. A famous ghost named Resurrection Mary is said to haunt the area and hitch car rides without asking.

Resurrection Mary first appeared in 1939, when she reportedly began jumping into cars near Resurrection Cemetery on Archer Avenue. After a brief ride, she simply jumped back out—right through the closed passenger door!

Soon there were other bizarre tales of Resurrection Mary's activities. The stories were always the same. At a local nightclub or ballroom, a young man would meet a woman fitting Mary's description: young, with blond hair and blue eyes, in a long white party dress and shiny white dancing shoes. The man would dance with her and notice her skin felt icy cold. At the end of the evening, he would offer her a ride home. The woman would accept and give him directions, telling him she lived on Archer Avenue. As they drove past Resurrection Cemetery she would leap out of the car and dart inside the cemetery gates. Who else but a ghost would call a cemetery home?

Resurrection Cemetery was renovated in the mid 1970s. Some people believe this disturbed Mary, because there were lots of Resurrection Mary sitings during this time.

The strangest one of all happened one night in December 1977. A man driving past Resurrection Cemetery happened to glance toward it. Just inside the gates stood a young woman. She was desperately clutching the iron bars with both hands. Concerned that the woman was trapped inside the cemetery overnight, the driver called police. But when police arrived, they found no one. Close inspection of the gate bars showed they had been pulled or bent apart. It looked as though someone had been struggling to escape. Even more chilling was a report that two small handprints had somehow become etched into the bars.

Will you ever see Resurrection Mary? That depends. Men see her more often than women do. And she's most likely to be out on a snowy or rainy night. Taxicab drivers seem to meet Mary most often.

In January 1989, a cab driver picked up a young woman passenger at a shopping center. Although it was snowing, the woman wore a thin white party dress. She seemed to be in a hurry and directed the cab driver to take her to her home on Archer Avenue. When they reached Resurrection Cemetery, she shouted, "Here!" Then she vanished into thin air.

Many people speculate that Resurrection Mary is

the ghost of a Polish girl named Mary Bregavy. In 1934, just five years before Resurrection Mary first appeared, young Bregavy was killed in a car accident in Chicago. She was buried in Resurrection Cemetery. Friends of Mary Bregavy reported that she did like to dance, but that's about all there is to go on.

Real or not, Resurrection Mary is probably the most famous ghost in the Chicago area. A song called "The Ballad of Resurrection Mary" has even been written about her.

Indiana
The Willard Library's Lady Ghosts

Location: Evansville, Indiana

Visit the Willard Library in Evansville, and you may find more than just books. Two friendly ghosts are said to haunt this brick-and-stone Gothic-style library. One has been nicknamed The Lady in Gray, and another is thought to be the ghost of Margaret, a former librarian in the Willard Library's Children's Room.

The first account of The Lady in Gray occurred in 1936, when a library janitor quit his job. His reason for quitting was certainly unusual: He claimed he'd seen the ghost of The Lady in Gray one too many times in the library basement.

Over the years since then, The Lady in Gray has reportedly been seen at the Willard Library by both visitors and employees. A security camera even spotted a ghostly form thought to be her. Witnesses describe her as wearing a long gray dress, high-topped buttoned shoes, and a shawl. Her hair is parted in the middle and worn in a long braid. She occasionally wears a gray hat and veil.

Sometimes people don't see her, but just sense her as either a cold spot of air or a strong perfume smell.

In 1940, the Children's Room was relocated to the library basement, where the janitor had first seen the ghost a few years earlier. A children's librarian named Margaret, who worked in the basement library from 1939 to 1989, supposedly often saw The Lady in Gray. She and the ghost became so friendly that The Lady in Gray followed her home while the library was being renovated in the 1980s.

On the library's one hundredth anniversary in 1985, the governor of Indiana held a celebration in honor of the library's "Resident Spirit—The Lady in Gray." In recent years, children have reported two ghosts in the Children's Room. The descriptions of the ghosts match those of The Lady in Gray and of Margaret the librarian, who died in 1989!

The Willard Library is on the National Register of Historic Places.

Iowa
Haunted Ham House

Location: Dubuque, Iowa

Do you like spooky organ music? How about lights that go on and off by themselves, windows that lock and unlock on their own, strange whispers, and creaky footsteps? If you like all of these things, you'll just love Ham House.

In 1857, a businessman named Matthias Ham built this twenty-three-room limestone mansion on a bluff overlooking the Mississippi River. Ham had made his fortune in various industries including lumber, farming, and mining. He even had his own ships to transport his products up and down the Mississippi River. One of his favorite pastimes was watching the river from a lookout high atop his three-story mansion. Bands of river pirates roamed the Mississippi in those days, stealing whatever they could from ships. When Ham spotted pirates at work one day, he alerted authorities. Angry at getting caught, the pirates threatened Ham with revenge.

Ham died in 1889 at the age of eighty-three. His

wife had already passed away, and most of his seven children had left home by this time. Only two of his daughters remained in the house. One night, his daughter Sarah heard strange noises downstairs when she was alone. Frightened, she wondered if the pirates who had once vowed vengeance against her father had returned.

According to legend, Sarah again heard noises coming from the first floor of the house a few nights later. She called out, demanding to know who was there. No one answered. Heavy footsteps began to shuffle up the creaky stairs toward her. Quickly, she locked her bedroom door and placed her lantern in the window to signal the neighbors for help. She grabbed her gun and waited in terror. When the footsteps paused in the hallway outside of her room, she fired bullets through the door.

When neighbors arrived, they found blood in the hall. A bloody trail led them to the riverbank, where they found the body of a pirate, who had been up to no good. Sarah had been right to fear pirates' vengeance!

The Dubuque County Historical Society began operating a museum in Ham House in 1964. Visitors and employees have reportedly experienced strange events there. Some people have seen a light moving through Ham House at night. Could this be the dead pirate's ghostly lantern? Perhaps he is doomed to forever retrace his path through the house on the night he died.

An electrician once heard organ music while

doing repair work at Ham House. This was odd because the pump organ in the house didn't work. In the upstairs hall, a window that is locked each night sometimes opens on its own by morning, and a light goes on and off by itself. Along the stairs leading to Ham's old lookout, inexplicable cold winds and icy spots are felt.

In 1978, a tour guide spent the night in the house hoping to shed some light on the spooky occurrences. Around three A.M., he heard whispering outside in the yard. He looked around, but wasn't able to find a soul lurking about. He heard strange footsteps and other noises in the house but could find no explanation for them.

For nearly 150 years, this beautiful Victorian Gothic mansion has stood along the Mississippi River. Though spooky sounds may echo through its halls, no one has gotten a peek at a single ghost in Matthias Ham House. Yet!

Kansas
The Blue Light Lady

Location: Sentinel Hill in Hays, Kansas

Cholera! Fear of the dreaded disease swept through Fort Hays as quickly as the epidemic itself in 1867. Elizabeth Polly and her husband, Ephraim, were unlucky enough to arrive at the fort at the height of the epidemic. The Pollys made their living by selling supplies to frontier settlements. Together, they traveled the Kansas prairie in a wagon filled with dry goods. But Fort Hays would be Elizabeth's last stop.

There was only one doctor at the fort to care for the many soldiers stricken with cholera. Patients with this infectious and often fatal disease had severe diarrhea and vomiting. Though she wasn't trained as a nurse, Elizabeth did what she could to comfort the victims. Everyone was so grateful for her kindness that they began to call her The Angel of Fort Hays.

Each evening, Elizabeth took a walk along the hilltop bluffs overlooking the fort. Her wide-brimmed blue bonnet and full-skirted blue dress could be seen blowing in the wind as she walked.

No one knows what happened to her husband, but eventually Elizabeth became fatally ill with cholera. Before she died, she asked to be buried on the hilltop where she had taken such peaceful walks. Her last wish was granted, and she was buried on Sentinel Hill.

But has Elizabeth's spirit remained in its grave?

Fifty years after her death, a Kansas farmer was the first to see what may have been Elizabeth Polly's ghost. The farmer was herding his cows toward the barn one morning when he saw a woman in an old-fashioned long blue dress and bonnet. She was walking toward an abandoned shack near Elizabeth Polly's grave. The curious farmer tried to approach her. However, his terrified horse refused to move one step in her direction. His dog ran for home with its tail between its legs. The farmer gave up and continued on with his cattle.

When he returned home, the farmer learned that his family had watched from a distance and had seen him encounter the mysterious woman. They told him that after he rode away, she had gone inside the old shack. His family kept an eye on the shack for the rest of the day, but the woman never came back out.

That night, the farmer and his brother-in-law decided to investigate. They rode to the shack and knocked on its locked door. No one answered. The lock was rusty, so the farmer gave the door a hard kick. It flew open revealing a dusty room full of cobwebs. It was obvious no one had been inside for quite some time—at least no one living.

The farmer later described the woman he'd seen to

an elderly man, who had once known Elizabeth Polly. The old-timer said the woman's dress and bonnet sounded just like those Elizabeth had been wearing when she was buried!

Around 1960, a policeman on night patrol may have seen Elizabeth Polly's ghost, too. As he was driving along a road on the outskirts of Hays, a woman in a long blue dress and bonnet crossed right in front of his car. She appeared so suddenly that he had no time to veer away. He felt sure he had hit her. The horrified patrolman screeched to a halt and got out of the car. He rushed to help the woman. But she had vanished.

Some years later, a man was harvesting grain on a farm near Hays. He could hardly believe his eyes when a woman wearing an old-fashioned blue dress walked right in front of his truck. He slammed on the brakes, and she faded away. A few minutes later, he felt someone watching him. He turned to see the woman standing in a pool of glowing blue light. Frightened, he looked away for a split second. When he looked back, she was gone.

If this woman in blue is the ghost of Elizabeth Polly, many wonder why she cannot rest. Some believe she is searching for the dead cholera victims who were buried near her grave but were later moved. Others say she simply enjoys taking a daily stroll as much as she did when she was alive.

Today, a limestone statue of Elizabeth stands in Elizabeth Polly Park in the town of Hays. The statue wears a wide-brimmed bonnet and long gown, and carries a bouquet of flowers.

Kentucky
The Many Ghosts of Mammoth Cave

Location: Mammoth Cave National Park, Kentucky

As if dark caves weren't spooky enough, Mammoth Cave just may be full of ghosts! Mammoth is the largest cave in the world, with 330 miles of tunnels on as many as five levels. Some spaces inside the cave are huge, stretching as wide and as high as two hundred feet. Other openings are barely big enough for one person to squeeze through.

In 1798, a bear hunter discovered Mammoth Cave. The cave made news when saltpeter was mined from it and used to make gunpowder during the War of 1812. After the war, hundreds of tourists began to visit the cave. It quickly grew popular, and millions of people have explored it since.

The most haunted areas of Mammoth Cave are reportedly the Church, Echo River, Purgatory, and Crystal Cave. While the identities of some of Mammoth's ghosts are unknown, those of others seem more certain. Three of the most famous ghost legends involve a cave guide, a Southern belle, and an explorer.

Before the cave became a national park in 1941, individual people owned sections of it. Some earned money by offering tours to visitors. Slaves often acted as tour guides before the Civil War. The best known of these was a man named Stephen Bishop. Bishop explored Mammoth Cave and drew extensive maps of it. He grew to love it so much that his ghost may linger on there and even occasionally join tour groups! Bishop's ghost wears white pants, a vest, and a wide-brimmed panama hat. This was fashionable attire back in 1838, when he was a guide.

And then there is the sad tale of Melissa, a Southern belle who fell in love with a Yankee named Mr. Beverleigh around 1843. Unfortunately for Melissa, he loved another woman. Miffed, Melissa decided to play a trick on him. She led him into an area of the cave known as Purgatory. But instead of giving him the tour she had promised, she ran off and left him there!

It shouldn't have surprised Melissa that Beverleigh disappeared. He had no light and didn't know his way around the cave. But she was quickly overcome with guilt and grief over the loss of her beau. Her ghost is rumored to wander the cave searching for him to this day. Some cave visitors say they have heard the rustle of her long petticoats. Others have heard someone whisper her name. Could this be Mr. Beverleigh's ghost, still begging in vain for her to lead him out of the cave?

Yet another ghost in the Mammoth Cave area is believed to be unlucky Floyd Collins, who discovered

Crystal Cave in 1917. Crystal Cave is located about five miles from Mammoth and is part of Mammoth Cave National Park. Collins went exploring in 1925 and got trapped in Crystal Cave for over two weeks. He was pinned under a huge rock, sixty feet underground. Efforts to rescue him made the news, and Collins became famous. But he didn't live to enjoy his fame. A sudden cave-in ended his life before he could be rescued.

There was so much public interest in Collins after his death that his body was displayed in Crystal Cave inside a glass-topped coffin. Tourists flocked to see it. Though his body was eventually removed, some say his ghost stuck around. If you are ever in the cave and hear a ghost calling for help, as others say they have, you'll know who it is!

Skeptics believe people see or hear ghosts inside caves only because their eyes and ears are playing tricks on them. Deep beneath the earth's surface there is no light and little or no sound. The rush of an underground waterfall might sound like the rustle of Melissa's petticoats. Faint bat squeaks might sound like Floyd Collins's ghostly cry for help.

Whatever you may believe, the hundreds of spooky sightings at Mammoth Cave have caused some ghost hunters to label it one of the most haunted places in the world.

Louisiana
Voodoo Queen Marie Laveau

Location: New Orleans, Louisiana

Need a love potion to make that special someone adore you? How about a voodoo doll or a charm to bring trouble to someone you dislike? In the 1800s, everyone in New Orleans knew exactly whom to see when they wanted such things: the undisputed voodoo queen of New Orleans—Marie Laveau.

There were other voodoo queens in New Orleans in the 1800s. African slaves had brought voodoo, a religion that involves magic and spells, to the city, and many continued to practice it there. But people from all races and social levels seemed to believe that Laveau was something special.

From her home at 1020 St. Ann Street, Marie Laveau sold potions, poisons, and magic charms to suit every need. She peddled charms to cure illness or cause it, as well as love potions and bags filled with magic spells. She led wild voodoo dances in an area of New Orleans known as Congo Square, and held pagan rituals with animal sacrifices.

It was even said Laveau once controlled the weather to please paying clients. When friends of two convicted Frenchmen approached her for help, she promised to stop the convicts from hanging as planned.

The day of the Frenchmen's scheduled execution dawned bright and sunny. The men were brought to the gallows in the public square. As the hangman's nooses were placed around their necks, a sudden storm swept in. It was so violent that the people who had gathered to watch the execution had to leave. The rain made the nooses slick, and they slipped off the Frenchmen's necks. The men fell unharmed through the gallows trapdoor. Afterward, Marie Laveau claimed she had kept her promise. The men had not been hanged as planned. (They *were* later successfully hanged, but Laveau had only pledged to save them once.)

No one knows exactly where Marie Laveau came from or when she was born, but her birth date was probably around 1794. People who saw her when she was in her eighties, said she looked unbelievably young. Had she discovered the fountain of youth? Probably not. More likely, there were actually two Marie Laveaus—a mother and daughter.

Two unmarked tombs in New Orleans' St. Louis Cemetery are believed to contain their bodies. It is commonly thought that the original Marie Laveau died in 1880 and was buried in St. Louis Cemetery Number One. Her daughter died ten years later and was buried in St. Louis Cemetery Number Two.

The legend of Marie Laveau is so powerful that

some people believe she still practices voodoo from the grave. They often visit the Laveau tombs to ask for help. Many of them mark tiny Xs in the dust on the tombs and leave offerings such as coins, beads, and flowers. They even leave notes with special messages.

It's not a good idea to knock on the tombs unless you're ready to see Marie Laveau's spirit. People say that three knocks will summon her ghost to rise from its grave!

Maine
Not Alive, But Still Kicking in Bucksport Cemetery

Location: Bucksport, Maine

There's an extra leg in Bucksport Cemetery! The bloodred outline of this human leg reportedly appears on a monument dedicated to Colonel Jonathan Buck, who was buried in the cemetery in 1795. His fifteen-foot-tall granite monument towers over the other graves and is a symbol of his importance as the founder of Bucksport. Legend has it that the monument has been cleaned repeatedly and even replaced in an attempt to remove the image of the leg. However, any such efforts seem to have been in vain. People say the leg returns to Buck's monument time and time again.

By many accounts, Buck was a well-respected, moral man. So why the leg?

One tale says Buck was once a judge at a witch trial and was cursed by a falsely accused witch named Ida Black. The woman was convicted of witchcraft and sentenced to death. At her hanging, she promised that one day her legs would dance upon Buck's grave.

In a slightly different version of this tale, the accused woman was burned at the stake. When her flaming leg parted from her body and fell to the ground, her son picked it up and hit Buck with it.

Some people don't think Buck ever presided at a witch trial. Most of the trials were over long before his time, and there is no evidence that a witch was ever hanged in Maine. However, others point to the fact that Buck once lived in Massachusetts, where the infamous Salem witch trials took place.

In yet another story meant to explain the leg, Buck was said to have unfairly convicted a man of murdering a woman and chopping off her legs. The story goes that the accused man cursed Buck, swearing that an image of the murdered woman's leg would someday show up on Buck's grave marker. The man claimed this would prove his innocence to everyone.

It is impossible to know which, if any, of these stories are true. No one even remembers exactly when the leg first showed up. However, it can supposedly still be seen on Colonel Buck's monument to this day, just below his name. Take a look at the leg if you're ever in Bucksport. You're sure to get a *kick* out of it.

Maryland
The Haunting of the U.S.S. *Constellation*

Location: Baltimore, Maryland

The United States fought long and hard to gain its freedom from Great Britain in the Revolutionary War. But after the United States won, they missed the powerful British navy. Because once its protection was gone, pirates from the Caribbean and North Africa moved in to attack American trade ships. U.S. trade vessels needed help, and fast. Congress decided to build six new ships to protect them. The first to be finished was the U.S.S. *Constellation,* and it is therefore the oldest ship in the U.S. Navy.

The *Constellation* was built in Baltimore, Maryland, and was launched in 1797. It had three mainmasts, thirty-six guns, a wooden hull, and was quick and easy to guide. Over the years, the ship served in many battles. Its crew fought against pirates, as well as in the quasi-war with France, the War of 1812, the Mexican War, and the Civil War. It became a training ship in the late 1800s, and was even used during World War II.

In 1955, after more than 150 years of service, the *Constellation* was finally decommissioned. It was retired to Baltimore and docked alongside a submarine named the *Pike*.

The *Constellation* turned out to be a spooky neighbor. People onboard the *Pike* heard odd noises and saw mysterious lights and shadows on the nearby ship. Some even reported seeing actual phantom crewmen pacing it's decks.

One night in December 1955, a U.S. Navy officer grew intrigued by the unexplained sights and sounds on the *Constellation*. He set up a camera and waited, hoping to determine once and for all who or what was causing them. Around midnight, he smelled the faint odor of gun smoke in the air and heard scuffling sounds. Quickly, he snapped a photograph. When it was later developed, the photo showed the glowing, hazy image of a sea captain carrying a sword and wearing an old navy uniform with epaulets! This ghostly captain has been spotted onboard the ship many times since.

The two other ghosts most often seen on the *Constellation* are a former crewman named Neil Harvey and his captain, Thomas Truxtun. Before the *Constellation* was even built, Truxtun was appointed as its captain in June 1794. The *Constellation's* first major mission under Captain Truxtun was to stop French pirates from attacking U.S. ships in the Caribbean Sea. On February 9, 1799, Truxtun and his crew defeated a forty-gun French ship called *L'Insurgente*. Truxtun became a hero.

But Truxtun was a hard taskmaster and was feared by his crew. When crewman Neil Harvey left his gun post during the battle with the French, he was severely punished. He was strapped to a cannon and blown to bits. This was a grisly way to die. It was, however, was an accepted manner of execution for the crime of leaving one's post in British and American navies in the 1700s.

The ghosts of both Neil Harvey and Captain Truxtun are said to roam decks of the *Constellation,* unable to forget Harvey's gruesome demise. In 1964, Harvey's ghost even reportedly gave a tour of the ship's lower decks to a visiting Catholic priest. As the priest was leaving, he thanked the ship's curator for having provided the knowledgeable tour guide. When the puzzled curator explained there was no guide onboard, the priest insisted an old sailor had given him a guided tour. The curator and priest went back down to the lower decks, but the mysterious tour guide could not be found.

Today, the *Constellation* is a national historic landmark and museum. It has been restored and can be visited at its location in Baltimore Harbor.

Massachusetts
The Witches of Salem

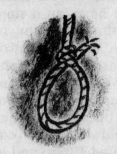

Location: Salem, Massachusetts

If you were accused of being a witch, how would you prove you were innocent? This was a problem faced by many people in Salem Village in the 1600s, after several young girls accused them of being witches. Back in those days, both ignorant and well-educated people believed in and feared witches. They thought witches acting on behalf of the Devil caused many everyday events. Vanity, dancing, or even making a joke might cause someone to be accused of practicing witchcraft.

The amazing story of the Salem witch trials began in the winter of 1691 at the home of the Reverend Samuel Parris. Nine-year-old Elizabeth Parris, eleven-year-old Abigail Williams, twelve-year-old Ann Putnam, and some other girls gathered there in the warm kitchen to listen to stories told by the Parris family's slave-housekeeper Tituba. Tituba was from Barbados, in West India, and claimed her former owner had been a witch. She told the fascinated girls all about voodoo and even tried telling their fortunes by reading their palms. If the adults in Salem had known, they would have put a stop to this. But the girls kept their meetings with Tituba a secret.

One day Tituba tried hypnotizing some of the girls. This was a disaster. It made some of the younger girls act strangely. When they began barking, meowing, and crawling around on all fours, the Reverend Parris couldn't help but notice. He questioned the girls until they finally said witches had caused them to act so oddly. They accused Tituba and two other women named Sarah Good and Sarah Osborne of having bewitched them!

Everyone was frightened and fascinated by the idea that there might be real witches in Salem. A huge crowd gathered at a hearing where the three accused women were questioned. Spooked by what they heard there, people began to suspect their friends and neighbors of being witches, too.

The young girls continued acting hysterically in the following days. They screamed, choked, and cursed as they went on to accuse others in the community of being witches. Once people were under suspicion, it was nearly impossible for them to prove they weren't witches. It was their word against the girls'.

On June 10, 1692, a woman named Bridget Bishop was the first person to be hanged as a witch as a result of the girls' testimony. Because she owned a tavern and dressed in flashy clothing—such activities were frowned upon in the 1600s—many were easily convinced she was a witch. Five more women, including

Sarah Good, were convicted of witchcraft weeks later and were hanged on July 19. Also among them was an elderly, beloved woman named Rebecca Nurse. People had become so afraid they were ready to believe almost anyone was a witch.

Altogether, about 400 innocent people were accused of witchcraft, and over 150 were jailed. Contrary to common belief, none of the accused witches were ever burned at the stake in Salem. However, a total of nineteen of them were convicted and hanged on Gallows Hill.

An eighty-year-old man named Giles Corey was among those suspected of witchcraft. When he refused to testify, he was executed in an unusually cruel way: by a method known as "pressing," where rocks were slowly piled on top of his chest. Throughout this process, his accusers demanded he confess to being a witch. He never did. Eventually, he was crushed to death. Today, some people say that if Corey's ghost is seen in the field where he died near the Old Jail, something terrible will happen soon afterward.

The Salem witch trials ended in 1693, after the girls declared the Massachusetts governor's wife was also a witch. This was too much for the governor. The girls had finally gone too far. The governor stopped the trials and freed everyone who had been jailed for witchcraft.

The ghosts of all nineteen people who were hanged as witches have reportedly shown up at one time or another at the Witch House in Salem. It was once the home of a man named Jonathan Corwin, who was a witch trial judge. Some of the pre-trial examinations of the accused witches took place in this house.

Author Nathaniel Hawthorne was born in Salem in 1804, over a hundred years after the witch trials. He was a descendant of one of the trial judges, and he had an interest in ghosts. Hawthorne thought his cousin's Salem home was haunted and wrote a well-known novel about it called *The House of the Seven Gables.*

Though it was once the scene of great tragedy, the historic area of Old Salem is a popular tourist attraction today. Every year, thousands of people visit the Salem Witch Museum, the Salem Witch Trials Memorial, the Witches Dungeon Museum, the Witch House, Gallows Hill, and the House of the Seven Gables.

Michigan
Great Lakes Ghost Ships

Location: The Great Lakes surrounding Michigan

So many ships have been lost or wrecked in the Great Lakes that these waterways may be overflowing with ghosts! Here are some of the phantom ships which reportedly sail the lakes on spooky nights:

One of the most famous is the *Griffon*. French explorer Robert Cavelier de La Salle built this forty-five-ton ship and first set sail in it on August 7, 1679. The *Griffon* headed west and eventually reached Detroit Harbor, Wisconsin, where it picked up a cargo of fur.

La Salle left the ship at this point in order to search for the Mississippi River by canoe. The *Griffon* began its return voyage from Wisconsin to Fort Niagara on September 18 without him. La Salle had made a lucky choice. No one knows what happened to the *Griffon* on its return voyage, but it never made it to Niagara. It simply vanished. Though a shipwreck that may be the *Griffon* was discovered in 1900, the ghost of this ship is still said to sail Lake Huron on foggy nights.

"The Wreck of the Edmund Fitzgerald," a popular

tune sung by Gordon Lightfoot tells of the tragic loss of the 730-foot freighter, the *Edmund Fitzgerald*. When this ship sank in a 1975 storm near Whitefish Bay, all of its crew were lost. To this day, some say the ghost of the *Edmund Fitzgerald* repeatedly attempts to cross Lake Superior and reach its Detroit destination.

The coal steamer *W. H. Gilcher* was lost in the Straits of Mackinac in 1892. Island visitors sometimes report hearing its ghostly foghorn during bad weather.

A mysterious ship captained by a French explorer named Sebastian sank in the Straits of Mackinac many years ago. Sebastian had once promised his fiancée that he would return for her—even if he was dead. He supposedly keeps his promise, visiting Mackinac once every seven years.

One of the spookiest Great Lakes ghost ships is a three-masted schooner called the *Erie Board of Trade*. Legend has it that the captain of the *Erie Board of Trade* disliked one of his crewmen, a man named Scotty. One day, he gave Scotty a dangerous assignment. Scotty was hoisted in a rickety chair hung from ropes to clean the tops of the ship's tall masts. It probably surprised no one when the chair broke and Scotty fell to his death on the ship's deck.

Afterward, Scotty's ghost was said to haunt the ship day and night. When one of the masts broke and killed the captain, a member of the crew claimed he had seen Scotty's ghost do it! The *Erie Board of Trade* disappeared during an 1883 voyage, and the ghost of this cursed ship is said to sail Saginaw Bay from time to time.

Minnesota
Guthrie Theater Ghost

Location: Minneapolis, Minnesota

Opera and theater events at the sparkling Guthrie Theater are popular attractions in Minneapolis. On performance nights, there is an air of excitement as ushers scurry to seat guests on time. Some nights, ushers may receive a little extra help from the spirit of a former usher named Richard Miller.

When he was sixteen, Richard Miller got a job as an usher at the Guthrie Theater. Miller was a shy boy who did not make friends easily. He had various physical problems stemming from a sports accident that made life difficult as well.

He enjoyed his work at the theater and even made some friends. But for a variety of reasons, Miller eventually became very depressed. One tragic day in 1967, at age eighteen, he bought a gun and shot himself. At the time of his death, he was reportedly wearing his usher uniform—a blue coat with a red patch on the pocket.

A few weeks later, an usher annoyed theater guests

in row 18 by walking around during a performance. During a break, they complained to another usher. He didn't know what they were talking about. There were no other ushers assigned to row 18. The pacing usher's identity was a mystery. Then the guests mentioned that the bothersome usher had a distinctive mole on one cheek. Richard Miller had had just such a mole. And he had once worked in row 18. The legend of the Guthrie Theater ghost was born.

A few ushers tried to contact Miller one night by using a Ouija board. (See Missouri section for a description of a Ouija board.) Their attempt probably started out as a fun way to pass the time. But when a message was spelled out instructing them to tiptoe into another room, they got a bit scared. They asked why, and another message was spelled out on the board: GHOST. Then the letters M I L—perhaps for the beginning of the name "Miller"—were spelled. Spooked, the ushers ended their game.

Two ushers slept in the theater on another night to watch over some malfunctioning mechanical equipment. Around one A.M., they noticed a cloud forming over the piano onstage. Suddenly, the piano began to play all by itself. When the cloud began to float toward them, they took off as fast as they could.

This theater phantom could be the product of overactive imaginations. Or it could really be a ghost. What do you think?

Mississippi
Nellie's House

Location: Columbus, Mississippi

Nellie Weaver loved her house so much that she lived there her entire life. Her father, businessman William Weaver, built the Italian-style house in 1848. It had two beautiful parlors, with chandeliers hanging from decorative plaster ceilings.

Nellie was a lively, educated young girl. She was an actress in local theater productions and was a favorite at parties. Many suitors must have admired her, but a man named Charles Tucker was the one who caught her eye. The two of them were married on February 28, 1878. To mark the occasion, Nellie used her diamond engagement ring to secretly carve her name on a windowpane in one parlor of the house.

Sadly, a few years later, life turned sour for Nellie and her young daughter when Charles left them. Nellie suddenly needed to earn money on her own. She opened a school in the servants' quarters of the house and taught some of her friends' children there.

Nellie passed away in the 1930s. Sparks from one

of the parlor fireplaces caught her dress on fire, and she died from severe burns.

In the 1950s, Nellie's house was renovated by new owners. They noticed that the name NELLIE had been scratched in the glass windowpane in one of the parlors. Sometime during construction, a ladder fell against that very window and broke it. The window had to be replaced, and Nellie's name was gone forever—or so it seemed.

Legend has it that some years later, one of the owners was in the parlor on a bright, sunny day. She happened to notice something scratched the window glass. When she took a closer look, she was astonished to read the word NELLIE. The name had reappeared in exactly the same place as before! How this had happened was a mystery. The owners hadn't done it. Many people wondered if Nellie's ghost had. After all, Nellie had once said she loved the house so dearly that she didn't want it to ever forget her.

Missouri
The Spooky Ouija Board

Many moons ago
I lived.
Again I come

Location: St. Louis, Missouri

Pearl Curran wasn't interested in ghosts. So she probably didn't expect much to happen when she sat down with a Ouija board on July 8, 1913. But the events which took place that July day and in the following years became the subject of worldwide amazement and debate.

Ouija boards are decorated with words, letters, and numbers that supposedly enable ghosts to communicate with the living. The board was invented around 1890, and some people think it's just a game. Others claim that when they ask questions, spirits actually move the pointer around the board to spell out answering messages.

Nothing so exciting had ever happened to Pearl.

As Pearl rested her fingers on the heart-shaped, three-legged pointer, it began to glide across her wooden Ouija board. To her surprise, a message was spelled out, letter by letter. It read: MANY MOONS AGO I LIVED. AGAIN I COME. PATIENCE WORTH MY NAME.

Patience Worth? Pearl had never heard of such a person. A visiting neighbor urged her to use the Ouija board to find out more. Via the board, Pearl learned that Patience was the spirit of a Quaker woman who had lived in Dorset, England, in the 1600s. She had sailed to America where she had been killed by Native Americans in Missouri. Patience's speech was sprinkled with old-fashioned words such as "thou" (instead of "you") and "hast" (instead of "have"). These were not words a modern woman like Pearl would normally use.

Pearl received many more messages from Patience through the Ouija board in the following days. Soon messenges were coming in so fast no one could write them down quickly enough. Pearl eventually trained herself to receive Patience's words without using the Ouija board. She learned to type information on a typewriter as rapidly as Patience could dictate it.

The messages Pearl got from Patience over the next twenty-five years were astounding. Altogether, Patience dictated about five thousand poems, several novels, and numerous short stories and plays. Pearl wrote them all down, and many were published.

Authors can spend a year or more writing a novel, and thousands of revisions are made during the process. But Patience wrote with a speed that was out of this world. She dictated *Telka,* a sixty thousand-word novel, to Pearl in only thirty-five hours! And Patience's words were published as written. No revisions were necessary.

Some people think Pearl was a fake, who wrote all

of the stories herself and simply passed them off as the work of a ghost. It's true that Pearl might have found it difficult if she'd tried to get her own writing published. The idea of stories being written by a housewife wouldn't gave been particularly unusual or exciting. But stories written by a ghost attracted lots of attention!

Other evidence seems to indicate Pearl was not a fake. Reporters and curiosity-seekers sometimes visited and witnessed Pearl writing Patience's words. Though only Pearl could hear the words, it did appear as though she was taking dictation rather than making up the stories on the spot. Additionally, Patience's novels were considered by some to be excellent literary works. *Telka* was set in medieval England, and the language used was accurate for that time period. Pearl reportedly had no schooling beyond the eighth grade and rarely read—it's hard to believe she could have written such a novel on her own.

Believers and skeptics alike debated the celebrated case of Pearl and Patience. A newspaper editor named Caspar Yost wrote a book about them called *Patience Worth—A Psychic Mystery.* Patience and Pearl became famous nationwide. Patience even had a fan club and fan magazine. When Pearl died on December 4, 1937, one newspaper ran the headline "Patience Worth Is dead."

No one has ever proven whether or not Patience Worth was real.

Montana
The Ghosts of Custer's Last Stand

Location: Little Bighorn Battlefield National Monument, near Hardin, Montana

In the late 1800s, the United States government wanted Native Americans to move onto reservations to make way for new settlers. When some Native Americans refused, the government sent soldiers to force them.

One famous battle over this issue was the Battle of Little Bighorn, which took place near the Little Bighorn River. It was also known as Custer's Last Stand, since it was a defeat for U.S. General George Armstrong Custer.

General Custer and his troops first encountered Sioux tribes led by chiefs Crazy Horse and Sitting Bull on June 25, 1876. Instead of waiting for help from reinforcing armies that were on the way, Custer began fighting. It was a disastrous choice. General Custer, 264 of his soldiers, and as many as 100 Native Americans were killed.

Today the battlefield is a park known as Little

Bighorn Battlefield National Monument. Over 250,000 tourists visit the park's monument, visitors' center, and museum each year. Some visitors sense intense sadness at Battlefield Cemetery, where many of the slain soldiers are buried. Several other locations in the park are reportedly haunted.

Custer and most of his men probably died in an area of the battlefield called Last Stand Hill. However, Custer's ghost seems to have wandered over to the museum. Some people say he roams the museum halls, serving as a sort of a night watchman. He checks to see that the doors have been locked, and keeps a lookout for intruders.

Spooky sightings have also been reported along the Little Bighorn River at Reno Crossing. It was here Custer's troops, led by Major Marcus Reno, retreated when they realized they were losing the battle. One of Reno's men, Second Lieutenant Benjamin Hodgson, was shot in the leg while helping wounded soldiers cross the river. He tried to crawl up a hill and escape, but he didn't make it. His dead body rolled down the hill to the riverbank. Over the years, dozens of people claim to have seen his ghost near a marker at the spot where he died.

In 1983, a park employee living near the battlefield may have encountered Hodgson's ghost in her apartment. She woke up one night to find the apparition of a man sitting in her living room. He wore a handlebar mustache and light-colored beard, and had terror-filled eyes. When she blinked, the vision disappeared. In an old book at the visitors' center, the tour guide later ran across a photo resembling the man she had seen. It was a picture of Hodgson!

Ghosts seem drawn to battlefields, but no one is sure why. One theory is that when a tragedy occurs in a certain location, the spirits and emotions of the people involved may somehow become permanently linked to the area. If this is true, it might help explain why battlefields such as Little Bighorn can seem especially sad or spooky.

Nebraska
The Musical Mystery Ghost

Location: Lincoln, Nebraska

According to a widespread tale, a woman named Coleen Buterbaugh once had a haunting experience in the music building at Nebraska Wesleyan University. It was around nine o'clock on the morning of October 3, 1963, when she first entered the music building. As part of her job as the dean's secretary, Buterbaugh was there to deliver a message to a music professor.

The professor was not in his office when Buterbaugh stepped through his doorway. But someone else was. A tall, thin woman stood next to a high shelf, reaching for some music papers with her right arm. She wore a long-sleeved white blouse, a dark ankle-length skirt, and old-fashioned shoes with buckles. The woman wasn't as transparent as one might expect a ghost to be. Still, she didn't move, and somehow Buterbaugh sensed she wasn't real.

The sounds of students practicing their music in other parts of the building faded into silence, and Buterbaugh smelled a strange, unpleasant odor. Then she happened to look out of the window. Instead of the other school buildings she should have seen, there were only fields. And it was summer instead of fall. The sun was shining, and flowers were in full bloom. It almost seemed as though she had been transported back to an earlier time, before the rest of the school had been built.

All at once, the vision of the old-fashioned woman disappeared. The scene outside returned to what it should have been: a gray fall day. The rest of the school buildings were visible once more.

Buterbaugh rushed out of the office. She was so disturbed that coworkers asked what was wrong. When she told them about the apparition, someone who had worked at the university for many years spoke up. He thought the woman she described sounded like one of the university's former music teachers, Clara Urania Mills.

Buterbaugh looked through the school's files and old yearbooks and found pictures of Clara. She *did* look like the woman Buterbaugh had seen. Clara had worked at the university, from 1912 to 1936, and for part of that time had worked in the room Buterbaugh had visited. Even more startling was the fact that Clara had died in the building on October 3, 1936, around nine A.M.—the same day and time that Buterbaugh had seen the vision!

Had Buterbaugh seen a ghost in the present? Or had she been transported back in time? Some people believe that all time exists somewhere. Normally, we can only see the present. But if time is somehow able to shift, time travel might become possible. Such a shift into the past could help explain what happened to Buterbaugh.

The Nebraska Wesleyan University music building was torn down in 1973, and the Buterbaugh incident remains a famous unsolved mystery among ghost hunters.

Nevada
A Silver Spook and Haunted Gold

Location: Virginia City, Nevada

In January 1859, a man named Henry Comstock made a huge silver discovery near Virginia City, which became known as the Comstock Lode. Some people think that after his death, Comstock's ghost returned to haunt his mine, the Ophir.

Legend has it that in 1874, a bright lightbeam shot sixty feet out of the opening to the Ophir mine. Townspeople gathered there, worried that the mine was on fire. If flames were to burn the wood structure supporting the tunnel, the mine might collapse. But to their surprise, the locals found no fire. Instead, they saw only the strange beam of light.

No one had the nerve to venture into the spooky mine that night. However, the next morning someone dared a young miner to investigate. The miner took the dare and was lowered into the mineshaft in the elevator. Seven hundred feet down, he got out of the elevator and walked along the horizontal portion of the tunnel. He heard a faint tapping sound and moved toward it with only a small lantern lighting his way.

At the end of the tunnel, he froze in his tracks. Standing before him was a ghost that appeared to be Henry Comstock himself! If it was indeed Henry, death did not agree with him. His skin was drooping from his skeleton, and his empty eye sockets glowed with a blue light. The ghost chased the terrified miner right out of the tunnel!

Another ghost—that of an outlaw named Jack Davis—is reported to haunt a treasure in Six-Mile Canyon, just east of Virginia City. Davis first showed up in Virginia City in 1859, along with many other miners who'd heard about the Comstock Lode. He soon owned a stable and a small gold mill, and began teaching Sunday school on the side.

But Davis had another hobby. He robbed stagecoaches and wagons transporting gold! He melted the stolen gold bars at his mill, claimed it was gold he had mined himself, and got away with it.

The law eventually caught up with Davis, and he went to prison for his crimes in 1870. Before long, he was released and was up to his old tricks. In 1877, he was killed while robbing a stagecoach.

When people heard about his death, some of them rushed to Six-Mile Canyon. They were hoping to find his gold, estimated to be worth hundreds of thousands of dollars. But Davis wasn't going to let anybody have his treasure, even if he was dead. When the first treasure hunters arrived in the canyon, his ghost sprang from the ground and shrieked at them. The men shot at it, but the ghost just sprouted wings and flew into the air.

This story seems fantastic, so it's possible the first treasure hunters on the scene made it up to discourage others from searching the area. If that's the case, their plan worked. Few ventured into Six-Mile Canyon after hearing their frightening ghost tale.

Many other locations in and around Virginia City are believed to be haunted. The ghost of a gambler, who shot himself after losing a card game, reportedly haunts the Delta Saloon. The ghost of a teacher known as Miss Suzette has been seen near the Fourth Ward Schoolhouse. The list goes on and on.

For such a small town, Virginia City has a lot of old cemeteries—as many as fifteen in one area. Perhaps it's no wonder so many ghosts are sighted there!

New Hampshire
The Ghost of Ocean-Born Mary

Location: Henniker, New Hampshire

Mary Wallace wasn't born at home or in a hospital like most people. She was nicknamed Ocean-Born Mary because she was born on a ship crossing the Atlantic Ocean. Though she lived to be ninety-four years old, it was really a miracle she wasn't killed within hours of her birth.

Mary's father, James Wilson, was the captain of the ship named the *Wolf,* which was bound for New Hampshire in 1720. The *Wolf* carried Irish immigrants hoping to settle in America.

Just off the Massachusetts coast, Wilson's wife gave birth to a baby girl. Shortly afterward, the *Wolf* was attacked by an infamous Spanish pirate named Don Pedro. Pedro and his crew looted the ship, and were about to kill everyone onboard, when they heard a baby cry. Pedro hurried to the captain's cabin, where he found Wilson's wife and her newborn child. He offered to make a bargain with Mrs. Wilson. If she promised to name her baby girl Mary—in honor of his mother—he would spare the lives of everyone on the ship. Mrs. Wilson quickly agreed.

The immigrants sailed on their way feeling lucky to have escaped with their lives. Mrs. Wilson kept her promise and named her child Mary. Ocean-Born Mary became famous as the baby who had saved an entire ship.

The *Wolf* landed, and the immigrants traveled on to build new lives in Londonderry, New Hampshire. It was there that Mary grew into a beautiful, six-foot-tall woman with red hair. She married a man named Thomas Wallace when she was twenty-two, and they had four sons. When her husband died after eighteen years of marriage, Mary suddenly needed a new home.

By coincidence, the pirate Don Pedro came looking for her at about that time. He had just retired from piracy and had built a mansion near the town of Henniker. Pedro had remembered baby Mary and decided to see what had happened to her. When he found Mary and her children, he invited them to live in his new house. Mary became his housekeeper for the next ten years.

Pedro probably didn't truly give up his pirating ways. He sometimes had strange visitors at the house and conducted business with unsavory characters. One day Mary found Pedro lying dead in the garden with a sword in his back. Many believed he had been killed in an argument over pirate gold, and rumors circulated that there could be buried treasure on the property.

Mary continued to live in Pedro's house until she

died in 1814 at the age of ninety-four. Her nickname, Ocean-Born Mary, was carved on her gravestone, where it can still be seen today.

For many years after Mary's death, treasure hunters and vandals were the main visitors to her house. Other people were curious and went there hoping to see a ghost or two. Some said that a spooky six-foot-tall woman with red hair peered at them from an upstairs window, or floated down the main staircase and walked outside to a well in the yard.

Mary's house fell into ruin, was eventually renovated, and is now a private home. Past residents have reportedly heard strange noises in the house and have said that Mary's ghost has sometimes helped them out of danger. But other residents have not experienced anything out of the ordinary.

At midnight on Halloween, the ghost of beautiful Ocean-Born Mary is said to make an appearance in the Henniker countryside. She rides the surrounding hills in a phantom coach drawn by four white horses, her long red hair flying in the wind.

New Jersey
Spy House Spooks

Location: Port Monmouth, New Jersey

There are no longer any spies at the Spy House, but there may be lots of ghosts. Perhaps two dozen!

Spy House got its name during the Revolutionary War because it was a perfect spot for Americans to spy on the British navy. When British soldiers visited this inn and tavern, American spies hid in the attic to eavesdrop. Once the Americans overheard which ships the British were from, they knew which ships had been left unprotected in nearby New York Harbor. They did their best to sink or capture them. The British began to suspect what was going on, and tried to burn the inn down. But employees put out the fire, and Spy House was saved.

British Commander Lord Charles Cornwallis often relaxed at the Spy House during the war. His grumpy, drunken ghost has supposedly been encountered in its hallways in recent years. Cornwallis has a right to be annoyed: After all, he was forced to surrender to the Americans at Yorktown, Virginia, putting an end to the Revolutionary War in 1781.

In the early 1800s, the Spy House became the hideout of pirate Captain Morgan.* Talk about cranky! Murdering, thieving, and kidnapping were nothing for this pirate. He once captured a French family and held them for ransom at the Spy House. When the ransom didn't arrive, he killed them. He may have hidden pirate treasure in tunnels leading from the cellar, but those are currently blocked off. Captain Morgan and his first mate are both believed by some to lurk around the Spy House.

Other ghosts who reportedly haunt the Spy House include:

☞ A tall man with a beard and a black hat, who surprises people by appearing behind them in mirrors.

☞ A sea captain's widow named Abigail, who occasionally stands near the house gazing out to sea in search of her lost husband.

☞ A group of happy children, who play tag in the backyard. The girls wear old-fashioned dresses, and the boys wear pants with suspenders.

☞ A little boy named Peter, who goes home with visitors he likes.

☞ A little girl named Katy, who plays in front of the house. She once spoke to a visitor, explaining how many years ago she was run over and killed in front of the house by a horse-drawn wagon.

☞ Native Americans, who sometimes attacked the Spy House in its early days. Their spirits peek in the windows. Are they looking for more victims?

The Spy House was built in 1648, making it one of the oldest buildings in New Jersey. It is currently a museum, which displays colonial furniture, tools from the 1800s, historical documents, antiques, and—if the stories are true—a couple of dozen ghosts.

Captain Morgan is not the same pirate as Henry Morgan.

New Mexico
Wild West Ghosts

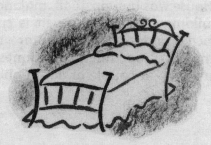

Location: Cimarron, New Mexico

The old guest register at the St. James Hotel reads like a who's who list of famous Wild West characters. Author Zane Grey is thought to have written portions of his western novel *Fighting Caravans,* at the St. James. Artist Frederick Remington, known for painting Wild West scenes, was also a hotel guest. Other visitors included Jesse James, Wyatt Earp, Bat Masterson, Buffalo Bill, and Annie Oakley.

Records show that at least twenty-six people were killed in the St. James Hotel and Saloon, which first opened its doors in 1880. In fact, there was so much shooting going on that the hotel's decorative tin ceiling had to be replaced in 1902. It had over four hundred bullet holes in it!

With all of the gunplay going on in the St. James, it's amazing that only three ghosts are reported to reside there. The first is said to be Mary Lambert, the wife of the hotel's builder, Henri Lambert, who was once Abraham Lincoln's chef. Mary is a friendly ghost who wants guests in the hotel to feel comfortable. She occupies her former room on the second floor. The fragrant smell of her perfume sometimes drifts along the hallways.

The second ghost is supposedly a gambler named James Wright. Legend has it he won the St. James in a poker game, but was shot before he could collect his winnings. If this story is true, it could explain why his ghost reportedly refuses to leave the hotel. He probably thinks he owns it! Spooky activities are said to occur in room 18, which may have been his former room. Sometimes, whiskey and playing cards are left in the room to entertain him and keep him out of trouble.

The third ghost thought to frequent the hotel is a gnome-like man called the Imp. This silly and sometimes annoying prankster likes to hang around the kitchen and dining room. When drinking glasses crack, pens disappear, or candles light by themselves, employees sometimes blame it on the Imp. Two men once claimed that a knife flew from a shelf to stick into the floor right between them. The Imp strikes again.

Today, the antique-filled St. James Hotel is a favorite with tourists. Guests—or ghosts, as the case may be— can sleep in any of fifteen restored rooms with Western-era names such as the Bat Masterson Room.

New York
The Fantastic Fox Sisters

Location: Hydesville, New York, east of Rochester

Imagine what it would be like if you could talk to ghosts. In 1848, two sisters named Kate and Margaret Fox claimed they could do just that. And people all over the world believed them!

Kate was only eleven and Margaret was fourteen when they and their parents moved into a small wooden house in the tiny village of Hydesville on December 11, 1847. The following March, the girls began to hear eerie thumping and knocking sounds in their bedroom. Neighbors told them that the people who had lived in the house previously had heard similar noises and had moved out because of them.

The unexplained sounds soon spread throughout the house. They went on all night, every night, and were so loud the family couldn't sleep. The girls' father tried to figure out what was making the racket. He searched all over the house, but the sounds just seemed to follow him. The girls' mother thought a ghost might be responsible.

One day, Kate and Margaret figured out a way to communicate with this ghost. When they clapped their hands, it seemed to reply. If they clapped three times, they would then hear three answering knocks. Before long, the girls worked out a code through which they could ask the spirit questions. If they didn't hear any knocks after their question, that meant that the spirit's answer was no. If they heard two knocks, its answer was yes. The spirit correctly answered a variety of questions, such as what the girls' ages were.

The spirit never actually spoke. It could only communicate by knocking. Still, the family was determined to find out who the spirit was, and eventually figured out a way to do this. They said each letter of the alphabet aloud and waited. If the spirit didn't knock, they moved on to the next letter. If the spirit did knock, they wrote down that letter. Then they started the alphabet again with "A" to find out the next letter in the spirit's name. In this way, its name was slowly spelled out: Charles B. Rosma.

Rosma claimed he had been murdered in the house and buried in its cellar by John Bell, a man who had once lived there. A former servant of Bell's admitted that a peddler visiting the house in 1844 had mysteriously disappeared. A search of the cellar was made. Pieces of cloth, human hair, and bone were found buried there. John Bell, who now lived in another town, was questioned. He denied murdering the peddler. There was not enough evidence to make a case against him, so the matter was dropped.

But because of Kate, Margaret, and their knocking spirit, many people had become convinced that it *was* possible to communicate with the dead. A worldwide spiritualist movement began, and the two young Fox sisters were the most famous spiritual mediums around. Powerful people such as circus owner P. T. Barnum and newspaper editor Horace Greeley invited them to visit. When the two girls contacted spirits in a public demonstration, hundreds of people gathered and paid a dollar each to watch.

Believers thought spiritualism was a new religion. Skeptics claimed it was all a fraud. They said the girls had not spoken with a spirit, but instead had somehow made the knocking sounds themselves. Others didn't care if Kate and Margaret could contact spirits or not. They thought the Fox sisters and their spirits were simply good entertainment.

In 1888, Kate and Margaret confessed that it *had* all been a fake. They said they had started the knocking to tease their mother, and had done it by popping their toe, ankle, and knee joints. Their game had spun out of control when outsiders had become interested in the knocking messages from their pretend spirit. The girls had been afraid they would be punished if they told the truth after lying for so long. So they had continued their deception.

Spiritualists protested, insisting the Fox sisters had been forced or bribed into admitting they were frauds. Both girls eventually withdrew their confessions of fakery.

Kate died in 1892, and Margaret died in 1893. On

November 22, 1904, a grisly discovery was made in the Fox family's old house. Children playing in the cellar accidentally knocked down a wall, revealing a secret hiding place. When the rest of the wall was torn away, a human skeleton was found. There were rumors that items belonging to a peddler were found hidden alongside the skeleton. This convinced some people that the skeleton was that of murdered peddler Charles B. Rosma. Had the Fox sisters been telling the truth all along?

Whether or not Kate and Margaret Fox were fakes will probably never be known for sure. The Fox house was destroyed by fire in 1955.

North Carolina
Headless Pirate Blackbeard

Location: Ocracoke Island, North Carolina

The infamous pirate Blackbeard has lost his head! So he's head-hunting near the tiny island of Ocracoke, off the coast of North Carolina. At least, that's what some people say.

Blackbeard was one of the fiercest pirates who ever lived. He was huge, standing well over six feet tall. His real name was probably Edward Teach, but he got his nickname because of his tangled, waist-length black beard. To frighten his enemies, he liked to decorate it with bones or even burning candles. Pistols stuck into a band across his chest, and a cutlass and daggers in his belt provided him with handy weaponry. He was always ready for action.

Blackbeard started out as a privateer on Britain's side during its war with France. He quickly learned how to attack and plunder ships. After the war, he acquired a ship named the *Queen Anne's Revenge,* sailed for the eastern coast of North America, and became a pirate.

One of his favorite hideouts was Ocracoke Island, part of a group of small islands strung like beads along the North Carolina coast. Blackbeard found it easy to lurk there and prey upon passing cargo ships. He was able to sell what he stole to local merchants. There was even a rumor that North Carolina's governor ignored his criminal activities in exchange for a cut of the loot. Blackbeard robbed and murdered anyone who got in his way.

Merchants and ship owners eventually grew tired of Blackbeard's troublemaking. They complained to Virginia's governor. The governor asked Britain to help, and they did. Lieutenant Robert Maynard of the British navy sailed to North Carolina and confronted Blackbeard in November of 1718. A tremendous sea battle commenced, with cannons firing and swords flashing. Blackbeard lost. It took five bullets and over twenty sword wounds to kill him.

Blackbeard's head was hung from the yardarm of the victorious British ship. His headless body was tossed into the ocean. Some swore that it swam around the ship three times before sinking. His gruesome head was later moved and posted at the entrance of the North Carolina harbor as a warning to other pirates. No one knows exactly what happened to it after that. One story says that someone covered it with silver and made into a punch bowl!

The Ocracoke Island cove where Blackbeard died has been nicknamed "Teach's Hole." Some people claim they've seen Blackbeard's headless body swimming there on moonlit nights. Others say they have seen him carrying a lantern as he wanders nearby beaches after dark. He has even been heard whispering, "Where is my head?" (One wonders how he whispers without a head.)

At any rate, Blackbeard's ghost probably won't have much luck finding his head. Nobody has ever gotten up the nerve to tell him that it may be filled with punch at a party somewhere. In view of Blackbeard's nasty temper, who can blame them?

North Dakota
The Crazy Cowboy of Black Butte

Location: South of Amidon, North Dakota

Yahoo! Back in the late 1800s, Bob Pierce was the fastest-riding wrangler on the H. T. Ranch in southwestern North Dakota. That was saying something, because the H. T. was the largest ranch in the state at the time and it employed a vast number of cowhands.

Pierce knew only one speed on horseback: breakneck fast. He was even nicknamed the "crazy loon" because of his wild riding style. The other cowboys on the H. T. valued their lives and were more careful.

While riding with an older cowboy one day, Pierce raced ahead as usual. Trying to keep up proved impossible for the older cowboy. When his horse eventually stepped in a hole, he was catapulted over the saddle horn and through the air. Although he wasn't seriously injured, the old cowboy was angry at Pierce for riding so fast. He shouted at him and proclaimed that someday his wild-riding ghost would probably gallop through the hills on horseback, howling like a wolf.

Though no one is certain, many people assume Pierce ultimately died in a riding mishap due to his own carelessness. Legend has it that over the years, his ghost has been seen riding right up the sides of Black Butte on horseback. No cowboy alive could accomplish such a gravity-defying feat. Black Butte is a steep, one hundred-foot-tall hill rising almost straight up from the ranch land plateaus.

If you're ever driving down North Dakota's Highway 85, keep an eye out for the "crazy loon." Some think the old cowboy's prophecy came true. On dark nights, Pierce's ghost is said to gallop to the accompanying sounds of wolves howling in the distance.

Yahooooooo!

Ohio
Tiedemann Castle

Location: Cleveland, Ohio

Is there a haunted castle in Cleveland?

In 1864, Hannes and Luise Tiedemann built their Cleveland dream home to look like a Gothic castle with turrets. They lived there for the next thirty-three years and the house became known as Tiedemann Castle.

Over time, some members of their family died at the castle. Their daughter Emma and Hannes's mother both died in 1881. Three more of the Tiedemann's children died in 1883. Hannes died in 1908, sometime after Luise had already passed away.

In 1913, the castle was sold to a political group called the German Socialist Party. For the next fifty-five years it was used for political gatherings, and was not lived in full-time.

In 1968, a married couple bought the castle. On the very day they moved in, their six children began to explore it. The youngest ones came downstairs several times to ask their mother for cookies. When she asked why they needed so many cookies, they replied that they were for their new friend. Upstairs, they had met a young girl, who was crying. Their mother went upstairs to investigate, but she never did see her children's mysterious new friend.

As the months went by, the mother reportedly became more and more disturbed by odd sights and sounds in the castle. The stomping sounds of a phantom army, possibly the ghosts of the Germans who once met there, came from the third and fourth floors at night. Organ music floated through the air, though the family didn't own an organ. On the third floor, a visiting friend saw a gray cloud drifting through the hall. When the visitor got too close to it, she almost passed out.

Though the father wasn't concerned about the possibility of ghosts in their home, the mother became so frightened that she began to feel ill. In 1974, the family finally moved away.

The castle then became a church. In order to raise money, owners of the church offered paid tours of the castle. Visitors sometimes had odd experiences there. One man heard his name called, and another had a tape recorder knocked out of his hands when no one else was around.

The castle's next owner was a police chief and his wife. No one knows if they encountered any ghosts, but they didn't stay long. They sold the castle after about a year.

In 1979, a man named George Mirceta moved in. He found the idea that ghosts might inhabit the castle somewhat intriguing. Mirceta conducted tours and asked visitors to write down any strange events they witnessed. Some tourists claimed they saw chandeliers spin when there was no wind. Some saw a woman dressed in black lurking in the high tower window. Others heard children crying when none were in the house. Could one of them have been the same crying girl the children had fed cookies to back in 1968?

It's impossible to say if Tiedemann Castle is really haunted.

Oklahoma
The Spooksville Triangle

Location: Miami, Oklahoma

You've heard of the Bermuda Triangle? The northeastern corner of Oklahoma has its own spooky triangle. But unlike the Bermuda Triangle, nothing disappears in the one in Oklahoma. Instead, things appear.

Mischievous dancing lights visit a triangle-shaped area between Miami, Oklahoma; Joplin, Missouri; and Columbus, Kansas. Sometimes there is a single light that is bright enough to read a book by. At other times, many dim lights appear together. Sometimes the lights are white. Sometimes they're multicolored.

The lights are picky about where they hang out, and can only be seen if viewed from certain angles or distances. They seem to prefer remote farm fields and back roads rather than crowded or busy areas. The lights will sometimes disappear at the sound of loud noises. One witness said that honking his car horn caused them to move away.

Many have offered scientific explanations for these lights (See Colorado section). The truth is that no one is sure of their cause. Some people think they have a ghostly origin. Legends tell of ghosts who have lost their heads somewhere in the triangle but can't recall where. The spook lights are the lanterns the ghosts use to light their way as they search endlessly.

One such tale says that one of the ghost lights is the lantern of a Civil War soldier. He died when he was hit in the head by a cannonball during a battle. Now he's looking for his missing head. One would guess that it's probably in bad shape after being hit by cannon fire. But we only get one head, so it's understandable if he wants his back.

Ghost lights have been seen in many places around the world. However, most of them don't stick around very long. The lights in the Oklahoma triangle are amazing because they have been reported for over a hundred years.

Oregon
Heceta Head Lighthouse

Location: North of Florence, Oregon

Lighthouses are usually built in isolated areas far from towns. So it's no surprise if they seem spooky or even haunted.

The purpose of a lighthouse is to save lives by warning passing ships away from dangerous coastlines. Shallow waters surround the rocky coast at Heceta Head, Oregon, and many ships had already wrecked there by the 1880s. Everyone agreed that a lighthouse was needed, so one was built on a bluff 205 feet above the ocean. It was named for Portugal's Don Bruno de Heceta, who had explored the area around 1775.

Today, the Heceta Head lighthouse contains a five hundred-watt automated light, which can be seen twenty-one miles away. But before the days of automated lights, lighthouses could not do their job alone. A lighthouse keeper had to live nearby to keep oil lamps burning in the lighthouse tower at all times. The first lighthouse keeper at Heceta arrived on the

job in March 1894. At that time, the lighthouse used a five-wicked oil lamp as its warning light. Keeping this lamp lit during a wild storm was dangerous work and demanded the lighthouse keeper's constant attention.

The nearby house where the lighthouse keeper and his family lived was called Heceta House. In recent years, caretakers in this house have noticed spooky goings-on. They shut cupboard doors only to later find they've been mysteriously reopened. Light switches turn on and off, and footsteps pound the stairs when no one else is in the house. One night, dishes in the kitchen cupboards began to rattle as though in an earthquake. The rattling stopped as suddenly as it had started with no explanation.

Another night, the caretakers were playing cards with guests. Without warning, a disembodied scream came from within the very room in which they all sat. Everyone, including their pet cat, was frightened by the cry. But it didn't happen again, and they had no idea who—or what—had screamed.

One caretaker reportedly even came across the apparition of a woman when he turned a corner in the hall one night. The ghost was dressed in a long skirt, but the caretaker didn't have much time to study her. She turned and fled, vanishing through a locked door into an unused room.

The strangest events occurred during repairs to Heceta House in the 1970s. When a carpenter was working inside the attic at a window one day, he spied the reflection of someone standing behind him. He turned around and was startled to see an elderly woman dressed in a long, old-fashioned skirt. Her manner of dress was unusual. But even weirder was the fact that she was floating several inches above the attic floor.

The frightened carpenter wanted to flee, but the woman was standing between him and the door. When she began moving slowly toward him, he got so scared he ran for the door anyway. He passed right through the woman as though she didn't exist!

The carpenter was soon back at work. An attic window had been broken, so he leaned a tall ladder against the outside of the house and climbed up to replace it. While working at the window, the carpenter suddenly glimpsed the same ghostly woman floating inside the attic. He climbed back down, packed his tools, and departed for good. Two ghost sightings were enough for him.

Later that same night, caretakers heard what sounded like a broom sweeping across the attic floor above their bedroom. The following morning they checked the attic. It appeared that someone had been sweeping, all right. Glass from the broken window had been neatly swept into a small pile. They were mystified. The attic had been locked, and there was no broom inside. But the marks of broom bristles were clearly visible in dust on the wooden floor.

Who is the floating woman keeping things ship-shape at Heceta House? Some ghost researchers speculate she may have been the wife of a former lighthouse keeper. Since it would have been part of her job to clean Heceta House during her lifetime, perhaps she cannot stop even though she's dead.

Heceta House is now on the National Register of Historic Places, and educational classes are held there by a local college. The attractive, red-roofed, white brick lighthouse tower is one of the most photographed lighthouses in the United States.

Pennsylvania
Gettysburg Ghosts

Location: Gettysburg National Military Park at Gettysburg, Pennsylvania

Altogether, over 600,000 American soldiers died in the U.S. Civil War. More than 50,000 of them died in the bloody, three-day battle at Gettysburg between July 1 and July 3, 1863.

The Civil War was fought between Northern states and Southern states, mostly over the right to own slaves. Soldiers from the North fought to end slavery and were called Union soldiers. Those from the South fought to keep slavery and were known as Confederates. Instead of the fifty states included in the United States today, there were only thirty-four states at the start of the Civil War. Twenty-three of them were on the Union side, while the remaining eleven states fought on the Confederate side.

In 1863, General George Meade led Union soldiers into the battle at Gettysburg against Confederates under the command of General Robert E. Lee. The Union side triumphed. Gettysburg was a major turning point in the war, eventually leading to the victory of the Northern states and the end of slavery in the United States.

Many of the soldiers who died at Gettysburg were buried right where they fell on the battlefield. There were so many dead bodies that it would have been difficult to move and bury each one quickly. Since the battlefield is, therefore, a giant graveyard of sorts, it's no wonder some people think it's haunted.

There have been reports that ghostly soldiers march on the battlefield in an area known as Triangular Field. Cannon fire accompanies these troops, who are called "the phantom regiment of Gettysburg."

A rocky area called Devil's Den is rumored to be haunted by the ghosts of Confederate soldiers from Texas who died at Gettysburg.

The ghost of a major in a gray Confederate uniform once reportedly appeared at a small stone house next to the battlefield. As it turns out, the living room in the house had been used as a makeshift operating room during the Battle of Gettysburg. Doctors had treated hundreds of wounded soldiers there. They had too many patients and little medical equipment, so it must have been a gruesome scene.

The weirdest ghost sighting at Gettysburg occurred back in 1863 during the actual battle. Union troops in the 20th Maine Division were on their way to join the fighting already in progress. When they reached a fork in the road, they didn't know which way to go. Fortunately, they got unexpected help from a ghostly guide. The glowing spirit of George Washington came riding to the rescue on horseback. Washington showed them the correct path, and the soldiers joined the fighting in time to help capture a strategic location called Little Round Top.

After the battle, this amazing ghost story spread among the troops like wildfire. There was an official investigation. A Union general, several officers, and hundreds of soldiers insisted they really had seen the ghost of George Washington that day!

Rhode Island
The Ghost Lights of the *Palatine*

Location: Block Island, Rhode Island

Just north of Block Island, a flaming ghost ship has been sailing the Atlantic Ocean for the past 250 years. There are many legends concerning this phenomenon, and most of them involve a doomed ship of Dutch immigrants named the *Palatine*.

Fierce winter storms hit the *Palatine* as it approached the New England coast in 1752. Food grew scarce, and the disgruntled crew mutinied, killing the captain and robbing the passengers. The crew made off with the lifeboats, leaving the immigrants behind to drift aimlessly on the ship. The tide eventually ran them aground at Block Island.

Block Island sits at the entrance to Long Island Sound, eleven miles off the Rhode Island coast. It is a treacherous area that has seen many shipwrecks, and pirates were always on hand to salvage them.

A band of pirates known as the Block Island Wreckers had seen the *Palatine* floundering. They attacked and plundered whatever loot remained on the ship once it reached shore. But then they had a problem on their hands: If government officials noticed the wreck of the *Palatine,* they might come snooping around.

In order to get rid of the evidence, the pirates decided to set the ship on fire and sink it. They told everyone onboard what they planned, and let the passengers disembark. However, one woman had been driven insane by the events of the voyage, and she refused to go. The pirates set the ship ablaze, anyway, and sent it back out to sea on the next tide. The woman's screams echoed across the water as she burned to death on the flaming ship's deck.

For centuries afterward, a mysterious burning ghost ship has been periodically sighted off the coast of Block Island. Today, witnesses still report seeing what has become known as the Palatine Light. Skeptics claim that this light is not a ghost ship at all. They think it is simply the result of gasses escaping from the ocean floor into the air. Believers disagree.

The Palatine Light appears at night, most often near Settler's Rock Grove or State Beach. It begins as an orange ball of light, which glows brighter until some say it finally turns into a flaming ship.

Ghosts ahoy!

South Carolina
The Gray Ghost of Pawleys Island

Location: Pawleys Island, South Carolina

Who needs a weather forecaster when you have the gray ghost of Pawleys Island?

Pawleys Island, reputedly the oldest resort town in the United States, has often been in the direct path of destructive hurricanes. Today's technology enables scientists to alert residents of approaching bad weather. But before hurricane tracking systems existed, devasting storms arrived without warning.

Fortunately, the island seems to have its own early warning system, known as the gray ghost of Pawleys Island. The gray ghost, named for his gray shirt, pants, and fishing cap, has warned islanders of approaching storms for the past 175 years.

The ghost made his first recorded appearance before the hurricane of 1822. He crossed paths with the daughter of one of the wealthy southern plantation owners who built summer homes on Pawleys Island in the early 1800s. The woman was strolling along the beach, when she noticed a man dressed in gray walking toward her. Suddenly, he vanished into the ocean. The following day a terrible hurricane swept across the island. It was the first instance in which a sighting of the gray man foretold an impending storm. Since then, the ghost has warned residents before the hurricanes of 1893, 1916, 1954, 1955, and 1989.

In October 1954, a businessman visited Pawleys Island with his wife. Though everyone knew a hurricane was heading for South Carolina, weather forecasters had predicted that it wouldn't hit the island. So the man and his wife had decided it was probably safe to visit. In the middle of the night, there was a knock on their door. A barefooted stranger stood on their porch. He wore a gray shirt and gray pants. A gray cap shadowed his face. The stranger warned them that the storm *was* going to hit the island. Then he disappeared. Frightened, the couple packed up and left. Hurricane Hazel arrived on Pawleys Island later that day. It was one of the most destructive storms in history. Luckily, the businessman and his wife had escaped safely.

Who is Pawleys Island's faceless gray ghost? Some believe it is Percival Pawley, the island's founder. They think he wants to protect residents of his island from harm.

Others think it is the ghost of a heartbroken man from Charleston. This man went to New York on business around 1800 and was shipwrecked on his way home. Believing him dead, his fiancée wed someone else. The Charleston man was rescued years later and returned to Pawleys Island for his fiancée. When she told him she was already married, he departed and died soon thereafter. For the rest of her life, the woman often saw a faceless man watching her from the sand dunes.

No matter who the faceless gray ghost really is, Pawleys Islanders are glad he's there to protect them.

South Dakota
A Wild West Hotel Haunting

Location: Deadwood, South Dakota

Back in the days of the Wild West, Seth Bullock was a go-getter. In 1869, he became a politician at just twenty years old. At twenty-three, he became one of the founders of Yellowstone National Park. By the time he was twenty-four, he was a sheriff in Montana. Along the way, he also tried gold mining and ranching. He even found time to befriend Teddy Roosevelt!

Bullock eventually moved to the lawless town of Deadwood Gulch, where he made the acquaintance of Calamity Jane and Wild Bill Hickok. In 1876, he became the first sheriff of Deadwood. Though it was no easy job to tame the town's gunslingers, Bullock's gaze was so piercing he often stopped fights by simply staring down the men involved.

Around 1895, Seth built the Bullock Hotel in Deadwood. It offered brass beds in each of its sixty-three rooms, a reading room, and a Turkish bath. Those were luxuries back in the Wild West days.

Today, Deadwood has been re-created to resemble

an old mining town. Historic buildings, museums, and other attractions draw many tourists to visit every year. Some of them stay in the Bullock Hotel, where, according to legend, the ghost of Seth Bullock hangs out.

Bullock died in 1919. In 1989, a psychic medium wrote to the owners of the hotel. He claimed that a spirit named Seth Bullock had tried to make contact. The spirit had talked of his friends Calamity Jane and Wild Bill Hickok. Strange? Yes. True? Who knows?

But in the years since, dozens of hotel guests and employees have reportedly encountered or sensed what some think is the sheriff's ghost. In 1993, two women were inside the hotel when they heard someone call their names. Yet there was no one else in the hotel with them.

Employees have heard unexplained footsteps when they were alone. Someone once saw the hazy shape of a tall man dressed in cowboy duds materialize. One woman was in the hotel by herself when she heard pans begin to rattle in the kitchen. She didn't want to chance meeting a ghost, so she hid in the cellar.

If you're ever in Deadwood and *do* want to meet a ghost, be sure to keep a lookout for a sheriff with a steely-eyed stare. ___

Tennessee
The Bell Witch

Location: Adams, Tennessee

One of America's spookiest hauntings took place long ago at a small farmhouse in Tennessee. There are many versions of the tale, and it's hard to say what really happened. But the trouble first began in 1817, when a farmer named John Bell came across a giant black dog-like creature with glowing eyes lurking in his cornfield. He was preparing to shoot it, when it vanished.

Not long afterward, John Bell, his wife Lucy, and their nine children began to hear strange noises. It sounded as though someone was scratching at the windows and doors of their house, trying to get inside. They checked, but found no one outside—at least no one visible.

Eventually, the spooky, scratching presence gained entrance to their home. The Bell children began to hear noises in their rooms that they thought sounded like a giant rat chewing on their bedposts.

Things got progressively spookier. Almost daily,

3C 38

BELL WITCH

To the north was the farm of John Bell,
an early, prominent settler from North
Carolina. According to legend, his family
was harried during the early 19th century
by the famous Bell Witch. She kept the household in turmoil, assaulted Bell, and drove
off Betsy Bell's suitor. Even Andrew Jackson
who came to investigate, retreated to Nashville
after his coach wheels stopped mysteriously.
Many visitors to the house saw the furniture
crash about them and heard her shriek,
sing, and curse.

TENNESSEE HISTORICAL COMMISSION

RE-ELECT

the family heard mysterious thumps, gasps, and choking sounds coming out of nowhere. Chairs sometimes overturned by themselves. Something invisible pulled the bedcovers off of the children as they slept, and pulled their hair.

At some point, the Bell family started referring to the spirit as a witch, and she became known as the Bell Witch. The witch began to speak to the family, though they probably wished she hadn't. She cursed, laughed, and screamed day and night. John Bell asked a minister for help in getting rid of her. The minister performed an exorcism, but it didn't work.

It wasn't long before the neighbors learned of the witch, and many of them came around to investigate. No one ever saw her, but many said they heard the Bell Witch's horrible cackling voice. Even Andrew Jackson, who would later become president of United States, reportedly stopped by. He left in a hurry when the invisible witch threw dishes and furniture at him.

John Bell's twelve-year-old daughter Betsy seemed to get the worst of the witch's torment at first. The eerie presence delighted in pinching and slapping her so hard that she had bruises. Betsy began to have seizures and fainting spells.

But for some reason, the witch grew to hate John Bell more than anyone. Because of this, some people think she may have been the spirit of an unhappy woman named Kate. Years earlier, John and Kate had become engaged, but then John had changed his mind. He had realized that she was too cranky for him to ever marry. Kate died mysteriously, and there was some suspicion that John may have murdered her, though that seems unlikely. If he *had* killed her, that would explain why her ghost might hate him. However, if Kate really had been a mean person while she was alive, perhaps she would have turned into a mean ghost, too. She may have just chosen to haunt John Bell for fun.

Whatever the case, John Bell became the focus of the witch's hatred, and she vowed to kill him. John began to twitch uncontrollably at times, and couldn't even get out of bed for weeks at a stretch. When he complained that his tongue was so swollen he couldn't swallow, a doctor prescribed a tonic. One night, his medicine disappeared and poison took its place. John drank the poison by mistake. He went into a coma and died on December 20, 1820—more than three years after the haunting had first begun. People said the witch was responsible for his death. She even attended his funeral, where she was heard to sing and cackle drunkenly.

In 1821, the witch announced she was leaving but would be back in seven years. In 1828—seven years later—the witch did seem to return to annoy the remaining members of the Bell family. After a couple of weeks, she departed again.

Some people don't believe the Bell Witch ever left the farm at all. They think she just sneaked into a nearby cave on the banks of the Red River. This cave is now called Bell Witch Cave, and spooky things are seen and heard there from time to time.

No one knows if there really even was a Bell

Witch, but something strange certainly happened at John Bell's farmhouse in the early 1800s. Frightened local residents later destroyed the house, hoping to banish the witch forever.

The Tennessee Historical Commission has erected a historical marker near the original site of John Bell's farm. In part, the sign reads:

According to legend, his (John Bell's) family was harried during the early 19th century by the famous Bell Witch. She kept the household in turmoil, assaulted Bell, and drove off Betsy Bell's suitor. . . . Many visitors to the house saw the furniture crash about them and heard her shriek, sing, and curse.

Before she left for good in 1828, the Bell Witch vowed to return once every 107 years. This means she should have reappeared in 1935, but there was no sign of her. Her next appearance should occur in 2042, if she keeps to her schedule as promised. But then, can you really trust a witch?

Texas
Remember the Alamo!

Location: San Antonio, Texas

The Alamo is one of the most famous landmarks in Texas. It was built as a Catholic mission in the 1700s, and was named for the cottonwood trees growing outside its walls. However, the Alamo is best known as the site of a bloody battle that occurred during the Texas War of Independence.

The state of Texas was once a part of Mexico. In 1835, Texans grew unhappy with the Mexican government. A war broke out when Texas demanded its independence and Mexico refused.

A Mexican army of four thousand led by General Antonio López de Santa Anna attacked the Alamo on February 23, 1836. On March 6, the Texans defending it ran out of ammunition. Mexican forces broke through the mission walls and won the battle. Many Mexican soldiers and almost all of the approximately 185 Texans at the Alamo died. Among them were famed frontiersmen Davy Crockett and Jim Bowie.

Santa Anna gave orders for the dead to be buried

in one mass grave and for the Alamo to be destroyed. Then he headed north, hoping to quash the Texas revolt completely.

Mexican soldiers began tearing down the Alamo as instructed. Things went smoothly at first. Portions of the Alamo were demolished.

But legend has it that as soon as the Mexicans tried to destroy the walls, something very strange stopped them. A disembodied voice thundered out, threatening that anyone who tried to tear down the mission would die a horrible death. Ghostly arms waving torches sprang from the walls. The Mexicans were no fools. They fled in terror, and the Alamo was saved from destruction.

Though the battle at the Alamo was a disaster for the Texans, it served an important purpose: It delayed Santa Anna and his troops long enough for Texas General Sam Houston to raise an army. Weeks later, Sam Houston attacked and defeated Santa Anna in a battle at the city of San Jacinto. Texas won the war, and a treaty granting it independence was signed on April 22, 1836.

Nowadays, the restored historic Alamo is open to tourists. Do its walls still thunder and greet visitors with waving arms? Some say yes, but you'll have to visit and find out for yourself.

Utah
Golden Spike Spooks

Location: Kelton, Utah, near Golden Spike National Historic Site

In the mid 1800s, there was a great race in the United States. The competitors were two railroad companies, the Union Pacific and the Central Pacific. One began laying new train tracks starting from the eastern United States, and the other laid tracks beginning from the west coast. Each company raced toward the middle of the country, hoping to make it there before the other one. Both tracks finally met at Promontory Point, Utah, and on May 10, 1869, a golden spike was hammered in. This officially connected the tracks to form one long, coast-to-coast train route. Cross-country travel in the United States became a breeze.

The hurried work of laying the tracks had been backbreaking. Many of the Chinese and European immigrant laborers had died in the effort. While laying track through Utah, Chinese workers had camped at Dove Creek. They lived in crude huts built over shallow pits dug into the ground. Because these pits looked a bit like sinkholes, the area became known as the Sinks of Dove Creek. The camps and huts have disappeared over time. But the shallow pits remain today as a reminder of the harsh living conditions the Chinese tracklayers endured.

Today, visitors who make the difficult trip to Sinks of Dove Creek may find more than they've bargained for: Legend has it that the area is haunted by ghosts, and even ghost trains!

In September 1979, a park ranger and some friends hiked to the Sinks and camped there overnight. For fun, they were reenacting a march that had been made over a hundred years earlier by soldiers in charge of protecting the railroad workers. Just as one of the soldiers had done in the 1800s, the visiting ranger stood guard along the rail bed at the Sinks as his friends slept.

In the middle of the night, the ranger was startled to hear the sound of a steam locomotive heading right for him! He could even see a train light flickering in the distance. But that was impossible. Though the long, flat bed where the tracks had once rested still remained, all of the tracks had been removed years earlier.

Still, the sound of the train grew louder. It seemed to come closer and closer. Then it was upon him. Though he never saw a train, he distinctly heard one whoosh by, belching steam and clattering along nonexistent rails. Suddenly it was gone, and all was silent.

The ranger was stunned. Before he could gather his wits, he began to sense he was not alone. He heard the low murmur of soft voices speaking Chinese. Then the tapping of footsteps surrounded him. Soon there was an additional noise—a loud, rhythmic banging. It sounded as though great hammers were pounding spikes into train track. The ranger even saw the flash of sparks this activity would have produced. But he saw no hammers, no tracks, and no laborers.

When the ranger rejoined his friends and told them what had happened, he learned that others had had similar experiences at the Sinks of Dove Creek. He was not the first to have had an encounter with the ghosts of the Chinese workers.

And back when the tracks were still in use at the Sinks of Dove Creek, train engineers occasionally reported a near miss with a ghost train. The ghost train would show up on their track, heading straight toward them. The engineers would slam on their brakes, but the ghost train wouldn't even try to stop. Certain they were about to die, the engineers would brace themselves for a crash. But nothing ever happened! The oncoming ghost train would simply pass right through the real train.

Boooooo-Boooooo!

Vermont
The Spirit Capital of the Universe

Location: Chittenden, Vermont

Did you know the spirit capital of the universe was once located in a two-and-a-half-story farmhouse in Chittenden, Vermont? In the late 1800s, over four hundred spooky apparitions appeared to audiences during amazing séances held in the house by two brothers named William and Horatio Eddy.

William and Horatio had special powers—or so their father, Zephaniah Eddy, claimed. Any powers they may have had likely came from their mother. Both she and the boys' grandmother were said to have had the ability to predict the future. The boys' great-great-great-grandmother had been condemned as a witch during the Salem witch trials in Massachusetts.

Strange things seemed to happen around the two brothers, even when they were children. Their father sometimes saw childlike ghosts appear out of thin air to play with the boys in the corn-fields. The two boys were banned from school because books flew through the air and mysterious knocks sounded on desks whenever they were around.

When the boys acted oddly, their father pinched or hit them. He didn't like their strangeness. That is, until he realized it could earn money for him. Zephaniah hatched a plan to have audiences pay to watch his sons' spooky antics, and took William and Horatio on a tour around the country. They performed séances in big cities such as Boston, New York, and Philadelphia. Their shows scared and upset many people. The boys were treated cruelly by skeptics. They were shot at, stoned, and nearly tarred and feathered in some cities. But as long as he was profiting from their shows, their father didn't seem to care.

After Zephaniah died, the brothers stopped touring and went back home to Vermont. But they didn't stop performing. They held séances at their farmhouse every night of the week except Sunday. Because of the Fox sisters (see New York section), there was a great deal of interest around the world in contacting ghosts at this time. As reports of the boys' abilities spread, spectators hoping to see them conjure up spirits came from as far away as Europe. By charging overnight guests ten dollars a week—a lot of money in those days—the brothers were able to earn a comfortable living.

Each night, the brothers seated their guests in wooden chairs around a stage on the second floor of the farmhouse. The room was dim, lit only by one kerosene lamp in a corner. A tall booth with a curtained doorway sat in the center of the stage. One of the brothers would go inside the booth and fall into a trance. And spirits would begin to arrive.

Before the startled audience's eyes, dozens of ghosts in all shapes and sizes appeared out of thin air. There were children, pirates, soldiers, well-dressed gentlemen, Native Americans, and strangers from faraway lands. All were wearing costumes, and many spoke foreign languages. Disembodied hands appeared and touched people in the audience. Tambourines floated around the room. This bizarre spectacle went on for some time, but each spirit eventually faded away. Once the ghosts had all disappeared, the show was over.

Were the spirits the boys conjured real, or were the Eddy brothers merely excellent fakers? Some people think the ghosts may have actually been the brothers dressed in costumes. Perhaps, but some of the spirits were small, blue-eyed women with babies. The brothers didn't fit that description. They were large men with dark hair and eyes. And how would these uneducated boys have known the foreign languages spoken by the visiting spirits? Where would they have gotten the variety of fantastic costumes they wore? We can only guess at the answers.

To this day, no one has ever figured out if William and Horatio Eddy's spirit shows were real or just clever trickery. The Eddy farmhouse is now a private home, with no outward evidence that it was once the infamous spirit capital of the universe.

Virginia
The Ghost Party at Michie Tavern

Location: Charlottesville, Virginia

There's a party going on at Michie Tavern, but only ghosts are invited. Or so some people claim.

Michie Tavern was built in 1784 and became a meeting hall for politicians such as Thomas Jefferson and James Monroe. The tavern also served as an important social gathering place for the nearby community.

On one special night, in the Michie Tavern's third-floor ballroom, the waltz was danced for the first time ever in America. Though tame by today's standards, the waltz was shocking at the time because men and women danced closely together. Everyone was horrified when a young, unmarried lady dared to waltz with a fancily dressed Frenchman that night. In the late 1700s, it was considered improper for an unmarried woman to do such a thing. There was an argument over her scandalous behavior.

Some ghost hunters believe that the party and argument which took place on the night of the waltz are re-created by the spirits of the participants on a regular basis. It's sort of a never-ending ghost party. The joyful sounds of music, laughter, and dancing footsteps are heard in the Michie ballroom, when there's no party going on—none anyone living can see, that is.

These days, Michie Tavern is a museum with a restaurant and coffee shop. It still contains much of its original furniture and implements, and looks similar to the way it did in colonial days. This should make ghosts from the 1700s feel right at home. In fact, some people say they have a ball there every night.

Washington
The Native American Princess

Location: Seattle, Washington

According to legend, the ghost of Native American Princess Angeline haunts Pike Place Market in Seattle, Washington. Angeline was the daughter of Chief Seattle (Noah Sealth), for whom the city was named.

Pike Place Market was built along Seattle's waterfront in 1907. Today it is a bustling market filled with hundreds of shops, restaurants, and vendors selling flowers, fruits and vegetables, unusual clothing, antiques, gifts, art, crafts, and much more. One tourist favorite is the fish market. Its employees delight in tossing fish through the air and making their largest fish "talk" to unsuspecting passersby.

In daylight, it seems hard to believe that this busy market is haunted, though some of the downstairs areas are maze-like and dim. At night, the market closes, and its creaky wooden floors and shadowy nooks begin to seem spooky. Suddenly it's not so hard to imagine the market is haunted.

For over fifteen years in the late 1800s, Princess

Angeline lived in a very unprincess-like wooden shack near Pike Place Market. Some Seattle residents thought her cabin was too uncomfortable for an elderly woman. They tried to convince her to move, but Angeline refused. She died in the spring of 1896, and was buried in a canoe-shaped casket.

Chief Seattle once gave a speech in which he said, "Our dead never forget this beautiful world that gave them being . . . They yearn in tenderest affection over the lonely-hearted living, and often return to visit, guide and comfort them." Some people think Angeline *does* return. Her ghost has been reported from time to time near various shops in Pike Place Market.

Photographs of Angeline during her life show her wearing a long plaid skirt, a fringed shawl, and a kerchief covering her grayish-black hair. Her skin was wrinkled, and she sometimes carried a walking

stick. Angeline's ghost has been described similarly. Witnesses say she always stares straight ahead, never speaks, and seems to float rather than walk. A white glow surrounds her translucent body.

At one time there was a guided tour that took visitors to other locations within Pike Place Market said to be haunted by a variety of ghosts. Some of these spirits included a former director of the market seen in the nearby library; a World War II-era man dressed in dancing clothes; an overweight woman barber who allegedly pickpocketed her customers before eventually falling through the floor of the market to her death; and a little boy who likes to play with the puppets in the market's puppet shop.

Pike Place Market has been designated as a seven-acre historical district, and many tourists visit and shop there every year. It is one of the favorite tourist attractions in all of Seattle. And it just may be a favorite ghost attraction as well!

West Virginia
Haunted Harpers Ferry

Location: Harpers Ferry National Historical Park, West Virginia

In 1861, the U.S. Civil War began. (See Pennsylvania section for more on the Civil War.) But years before the war, a famous battle over slavery was fought at Harpers Ferry. It all started with a plan cooked up by an abolitionist from Kansas named John Brown. He hated slavery, and decided to do something about it.

In October 1859, Brown gathered a small group of about twenty followers. They raided the Harpers Ferry arsenal, where government weapons were made and stored. Brown hoped to capture the weapons and give them to slaves on nearby plantations. According to his plan, these slaves would then fight to free other slaves in a nationwide slave rebellion.

At first, it seemed his plan would succeed. He captured the armory. But it wasn't long before Colonel Robert E. Lee's soldiers recaptured it. Brown was arrested and put on trial for treason. He was convicted in

November and was hanged on December 2, 1859. This angered many abolitionists from the North. But other people believed it was a fair punishment because Brown had broken the law by attacking a federally-owned building.

Today, Harpers Ferry is a national park, where tour guides dressed in colonial costume tell visitors about the history of the area.

Rumor has it that Brown's ghost likes to mingle with tourists and has even posed for pictures with them! One family believes they met him while touring Harpers Ferry. They had no idea he might be a ghost, and asked him to be part of their group photo. They thought it would be funny to include him in a picture of Harpers Ferry because he looked like John Brown. Their photograph came out perfectly, except for one detail: There was a blank space where the John Brown look-alike had been standing. He didn't appear in their picture, even though he had actually posed for it!

John Brown's white-haired ghost is also sometimes seen walking past storefronts on the park's streets. He goes only as far as the firehouse, where he then disappears.

Before he led his doomed raid, Brown stayed in a farmhouse about five miles outside of Harpers Ferry. Some people say that the ghosts of him and his men haunt this house today. Witnesses have reported unexplained snores, whispers, and the sound of footsteps on the stairs.

Though John Brown's raid was a failure, it did

help bring the issue of slavery to national attention. He became famous, and abolitionists wrote a song about him called "John Brown's Body." It goes something like this: "John Brown's body lies a-moulderin' in the grave. . ." It's not a happy song. However, John Brown would undoubtedly be very happy to know that slavery *was* finally abolished at the end of the Civil War.

Wisconsin
The Hanging Ghost of Walker House

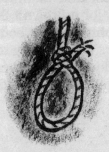

Location: Mineral Point, Wisconsin

People in Wisconsin couldn't stop talking about William Caffee's hanging on November 1, 1842. Caffee had been convicted of shooting another man, and he was to be hanged in the front yard of a log inn known as Walker House. The hanging was big news in the small town of Mineral Point, which was home to lead miners, cowboys, pioneers, and politicians. A crowd of nearly four thousand people gathered to watch the exciting event. Some even brought picnic lunches.

Understandably, William Caffee didn't share their enthusiasm. He felt nothing but contempt for his audience, and decided to show it. Caffee jumped on the casket that sat waiting for his dead body, and pretended to ride it like a horse. He grabbed two beer bottles and drummed a funeral march on the casket's sides. Despite his antics, Caffee did hang that day. Though his body was buried elsewhere, some believe his spirit never left Walker House.

Years after Caffee's death, Walker House stood vacant. It changed hands a few times before a new owner finally purchased it in the 1970s. Inn employees wondered if ghosts were in residence when strange things allegedly began to occur: Some employees heard disembodied voices. One man even had conversations with someone invisible. Pots and pans swayed back and forth and crashed together when no one was in the kitchen. An invisible prankster lifted waitresses' hair above their heads. A bartender heard heavy breathing and footsteps when he was alone in the second-floor bar. Guests heard footsteps coming from the bar when it was empty of people. Doors at the inn sometimes locked and unlocked by themselves.

As if all of that wasn't odd enough, something even more bizarre eventually happened. In 1981, an inn employee met a stranger sitting on an upstairs porch. The stranger was dressed in dusty jeans and looked like an old miner. He wore a black felt hat on his shoulders. He couldn't wear it on his head like a normal person because this man was headless! The employee had heard the story of William Caffee's hanging and immediately wondered if this might be Caffee's ghost. He didn't get a chance to ask, because the headless man quickly vanished.

The ghost at the inn seems most restless when large groups of people are visiting. Perhaps Caffee's ghost recalls the gawkers who once gathered at his hanging. He may be letting everyone know that, for him, crowds are just one big "pain in the neck."

Wyoming
Frontier Fort Phantoms

Location: The Fort Laramie National Historic Site at Fort Laramie, Wyoming

From 1834 to 1890, Fort Laramie was a favorite pit stop for pioneers heading west along the Oregon Trail. While wagon trains rested and loaded up with fresh supplies, soldiers at the fort protected them from Native American attacks and other dangers.

In recent years, Fort Laramie has been preserved as a national historic site for tourists to enjoy. However, several areas of the fort are said to be haunted by images from the past.

The army barracks where soldiers once lived is still alive and stomping, according to some witnesses. The sound of heavy boots pounding along the walkway can sometimes be heard there at dawn. When the fort was active, soldiers were awakened each morning by a trumpet sounding reveille. They hurried to fall into line, each wearing a pair of sturdy army boots. A ghostly replay of this exercise could account for the recurring stomping noises on the boardwalk.

A two-story building called the Captain's Quarters seems to be haunted by a ghost, who has been nicknamed George. George likes to play harmless pranks. His bony fingers sometimes touch visitors' arms or tap them on the shoulder. A caretaker once reported that someone or something grabbed him in the Captain's Quarters. He whirled around to see who it was, but no one was there.

Part of the caretaker's job is to lock the doors at the front and back of the Captain's Quarters at the end of each day. One night, the caretaker locked the dead bolt on one door and then went around and locked the other door as usual. When he returned to the first door, he found it unlocked and standing wide open! After this happened more than once, the caretaker decided to try talking George out of playing pranks. This seemed to work for the most part, but every now and then George gets up to his old tricks again.

Another building on the fort's grounds, called Old Bedlam, may also be haunted. It was built in 1849, and became the fort's headquarters. Meetings among important military officials took place there. And perhaps meetings among ghosts still do.

In the 1980s, two fort employees were talking and laughing together on the upstairs outside balcony of Old Bedlam. Suddenly, they heard someone bang on the window of the adjoining meeting room. Inside the window stood an army officer. He asked them to be quiet because there was a meeting going on in the room. Then he vanished right before their eyes.

Back in 1871, an army officer spotted a legendary

ghost outside of the fort walls. He was hunting when he saw a beautiful, dark-haired young woman racing along on a black stallion. The officer thought she might be in trouble, so he rode after her. But when they both reached the top of a hill, the woman disappeared. She couldn't have ridden out of sight, because the flat plain stretched out in all directions as far as he could see. There was no place to hide.

The officer later told others what had happened, and learned that the woman had been seen before. She was commonly thought to be the ghost of an officer's daughter, who had lived at the fort when it was a fur-trading center. Even though it was dangerous to ride outside of the fort walls, the woman had defied her father one day and done it, anyway. She was never seen alive again.

Her ghost is known as "the lady in green" because of the brilliant green riding habit, feathered hat, and veil she wears. She only rides once every seven years, so be on the lookout. Her next trips should take place in 2004 and 2011!

Alberta, Canada
The Bellhop and the Bride at the Banff Springs Hotel

Location: Banff, in the Canadian province of Alberta

If you buzz for a bellhop at the Banff Springs Hotel, will a ghost show up to carry your luggage? Good question.

The Banff Springs Hotel was built in 1888 in the heart of Banff National Park in the Canadian Rocky Mountains. The Canadian Pacific Railway built this hotel and others across Canada to encourage tourist travel on their new railroad in the late 1800s. This magnificent hotel, designed to resemble a Scottish castle, is eleven stories high and has 829 rooms, many with lovely mountain views.

Hotel guests have been treated to every luxury imaginable over the years. The hotel has shops, a bowling alley, a sauna and gym, as well as golf, tennis, and horseback riding. Its efficient staff of bellhops is always ready to carry luggage or help with problems.

A Scotsman named Sam McCauley was the hotel's head bellhop at one time. Before his death in 1969, he sometimes said he would come back and help out at the hotel after he died. Rumor has it that he has kept his promise.

Years after Sam's death, guests reported that a bellhop fitting his description helped carry their luggage. People began to suspect Sam was back at work.

When two women were locked out of their room one day, they called the hotel desk for help. By the time the bellhop arrived to assist, their door had already been unlocked. An elderly bellhop with white hair, who wore a uniform with a double-breasted plaid jacket, had done the job. Such old-fashioned uniforms were once worn by the bellhops. But they have since been replaced with more modern ones. Sam again?

Another ghost reported at the hotel is a lonely bride who waltzes near the Rob Roy dining room. She is said to be the ghost of a woman who died at the hotel on her wedding day long ago. As she was descending the spiral staircase, her wedding gown caught fire from a candle. One story says she then fell to her death at the bottom of the stairs. Another says she burned to death. After this unhappy event, the staircase was walled off, but it has recently been reopened.

Several other ghosts are thought to haunt the Banff Springs Hotel. The ghosts of legend seem harmless and lend an atmosphere of intrigue to the hotel. It is even rumored that author Stephen King was inspired to write his novel *The Shining* after visiting the Banff Springs Hotel. Talk about spooky!

British Columbia, Canada
Springtime Spirits

Location: Oak Bay in Victoria, in the Canadian province of British Columbia

Beautiful Oak Bay doesn't seem haunted. But is it?

In 1936, Oak Bay was the scene of a mysterious tragedy. A man allegedly killed his estranged wife after a meeting with her at the Oak Bay Beach Hotel. Her body was discovered days later at the nearby Victoria Golf Course. A hunt began for her husband, and his lifeless body was found floating in Oak Bay. There was speculation that he had jumped from the rocks and drowned himself after murdering his wife. But murder-suicide was never proven.

Things were quiet for many years afterward. Rather suddenly in the 1960s, someone reported seeing the ghost of the dead woman! She was standing along the edge of the rocky outcropping from which her husband had once leaped, fallen, or been pushed into the sea below.

After that, others sometimes saw a woman running along the beach. She was described as a hazy gray figure floating just above the rocks. She wore a white dress, possibly a wedding gown. The woman always did the same thing. When she reached the edge of the rocks, she would peer into the sea below. She seemed to be searching for her lost husband. Were she to ever find him, it's hard to guess what she might do or say to him. Her attitude probably depends on whether he actually did kill her or not.

The ghostly woman is most often seen in the spring, which is the time of year the two tragic deaths occurred.

Nova Scotia, Canada
The Amherst Poltergeist

Location: Amherst, in the Canadian province of Nova Scotia

ESTHER COX, YOU ARE MINE TO KILL. On September 10, 1878, those frightening words were scrawled in huge letters on the bedroom wall of a nineteen-year-old woman named Esther Cox. Legend has it that the message was the work of the Amherst Demon, possibly the most famous poltergeist in Canadian history.

Young Esther Cox lived in the two-story home of her sister Olive and her sister's husband, Daniel Teed, in the town of Amherst. Other family members lived in the crowded house as well, amounting to a total of eight people.

The poltergeist first arrived at the home shortly after Esther had been threatened and terrified by a local boy named Bob. Coincidence? Maybe not. Researchers theorize that her distress over this incident may have created an atmosphere which invited poltergeist activity.

During the night of September 4, 1878, the haunting

began. While sleeping, Esther felt something strange touch her leg. She jumped from the bed she shared with her sister Jennie. The next night, the girls heard odd scratching sounds under their bed. The third night, Esther awoke suffering from a strange illness. Her arms and legs swelled, and her eyes bulged from their sockets. Suddenly there was a loud crash, and Esther's illness disappeared as quickly as it had begun. On the fourth night, covers flew off the girls' bed, as though grabbed by unseen hands. The mysterious swelling struck Esther once again. She returned to normal instantly at the sound of a thundering crash, just as had happened the night before.

A doctor was called in to examine Esther. He supposedly witnessed unexplained knocking as well as the writing of the chilling threat: ESTHER COX, YOU ARE MINE TO KILL. At times during his visit, the house walls shook so hard that plaster broke away and fell to the floor.

In the doctor's opinion, Esther didn't seem to be faking her illness or somehow causing trouble to get attention. Still, he didn't have a cure. All he could do was sedate her to keep her calm.

Sometime later, Esther became ill with diphtheria. Fortunately, the poltergeist left her alone while she was sick. Once she recovered, Esther went to visit another sister in New Brunswick. The poltergeist disappeared, and all was well for a time.

Then Esther returned home to Amherst. Big mistake. The spirit came back and threatened to burn the house down. The entire family was kept busy during the following days putting out small fires that set spontaneously all over the house. Since Esther's presence seemed to attract the troublemaker, she was forced to leave for the safety of her family. She moved from place to place for months, living with friends or working at various jobs. A couple in the country invited her to take a job as their servant at one point. But soon after she went to live with them, their barn burned down. Esther was arrested, convicted of arson, and she served one month in jail. Some people believed she had set the fire, but others blamed it on the poltergeist.

Around this time, an American magician named Walter Hubbell visited Esther to learn more about the haunting. He decided there was money to be made by having her give public performances in which the poltergeist would do tricks. He advertised Esther as "the girl with the devils in her." Esther's stage career was short-lived. The poltergeist would not perform on command, so audiences were disappointed.

Eventually, the poltergeist left for good. There was some talk that a Native American medicine man had performed an exorcism and driven the demon away. Whatever the case, Esther Cox lived the rest of her life in peace. She moved to the United States, married, and died at age fifty-two.

The baffling case of Esther Cox and the Amherst poltergeist has never been solved. The house in which Esther once lived has disappeared and a store now occupies the site. Magician Walter Hubbell wrote a book about his experiences with Esther titled *The Great Amherst Mystery.* It became a best-seller, and the Amherst Demon became a legend.

Ontario, Canada
Not-Haunted, Haunted Mackenzie House

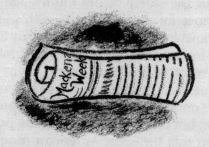

Location: Toronto, in the Canadian province of Ontario, Canada

The Toronto Historical Board operates a museum in Mackenzie House and doesn't think it's haunted. But some people believe otherwise. In fact, the three-story brick mansion at 82 Bond Street is sometimes called one of Canada's most haunted houses.

The house is named after William Lyon Mackenzie, Toronto's first mayor, who is one of the ghosts rumored to haunt it. Mackenzie moved to Canada from Scotland in 1820, and began publishing a newspaper called *The Colonial Advocate*. He was critical of the government, and his radical views got him into trouble more than once. Mackenzie was elected to the Canadian Legislative Assembly, was repeatedly expelled, and was eventually kicked out altogether. However, he was popular with the general public, who elected him mayor of Toronto in 1834.

Mackenzie grew increasingly unhappy with the Canadian government and finally led seven hundred followers in a rebellion against it in 1837. His attempt was a failure. He was convicted of treason but later pardoned. He began another newspaper, called *Mackenzie's Weekly Message,* which he published until 1860.

Mackenzie moved into Mackenzie House in 1859 and died there just two years later in a second-floor bedroom. His wife, Isabel, died in 1873.

In the 1950s and 1960s, rumors of ghosts began to circulate. Mackenzie's ghost was supposedly heard to operate his old printing press in the cellar of the house. Piano music was heard when there was no one at the piano. A vision of Mackenzie once visited the house's caretakers in the dead of night. Isabel Mackenzie was sometimes heard hurrying down the stairs and out the front door. She even once supposedly slapped one of the caretakers, giving her a black eye.

In 1960, an exorcism was reportedly performed to rid the house of any lingering ghosts. Did it work? Opinions on that spooky question differ.

What Do You Think?

Some of the tales in this book are spooky. Others are strange. But no one really knows if they are true. With each retelling of a ghost story, the facts may change until more than one version evolves. This book includes just one version of each tale, but there may be others as well. Decide for yourself if you think the ghosts and other spirits in this book are (or once were) real.

A Spooky Warning

Many of the sites mentioned in this book welcome tourists for a fee. Consult travel and tourism guides, convention and visitors bureaus, and chambers of commerce to find out which locations welcome visitors.

Many locations in this book are publicly or privately owned, do not welcome curiosity-seekers, and should absolutely not be visited.

Never go ghost hunting or visit a spooky site without the permission and supervision of your parents or an adult guardian. Never disturb or destroy anything at a site. Some of the locations mentioned in this book may be too isolated, dangerous, or hazardous to visit safely. Always research and ask locally for information about destinations before you visit them. And always use caution and good judgment!

Spooky Words

Apparition— a ghost that can be seen

Exorcist— a person who performs a religious ritual to try to drive out an evil spirit

Ghost— the spirit of a dead person or animal that may appear in various forms, such as a transparent mist or a solid figure

Ghoul— an evil ghost or demon

Haunt— to visit often

Haunting— when a ghost appears at the same place again and again

Ouija board— (pronounced Wee-ja)—A flat board with letters, numbers, and words printed on it. When used in combination with a pointer, some people believe that users can communicate with spirits.

Phantom— a ghost that can be seen

Poltergeist— a noisy spirit that may be a troublemaker

Psychic— a person who believes he or she can sense the presence of ghosts and other supernatural beings or forces

Séance— a meeting for the purpose of communicating with ghosts or spirits

Skeptic— someone who does not believe information until it is proven to be absolutely true

Spirit— a life-giving force or soul; a ghost

Spiritual— medium a person who claims to be able to speak with ghosts or spirits of the dead

Spook— a slang term for a ghost

Trance— a dazed, sleeplike state during which some spiritual mediums claim to be able to communicate with spirits of the dead

Voodoo— a religion that began in Africa, which may involve charms, spells, and voodoo dolls

Witch— someone who practices sorcery and claims to have magic powers

Selected References

Batten, Mary. *The 25 Scariest Hauntings in the World.* Los Angeles, California: Lowell House Juvenile, 1996.

Blackman, W. Haden. *The Field Guide to North American Hauntings.* New York, New York: Three Rivers Press, 1998.

Cohen, Daniel. *Ghost in the House.* New York, New York: Dutton Children's Books, 1993.

Elfman, Eric. *The Very Scary Almanac.* New York, New York: Random House, 1993.

Emert, Phyllis. *The 25 Scariest Places in the World.* Los Angeles, California: Lowell House, 1995.

MacDonald, Margaret Read. *Ghost Stories from the Pacific Northwest.* Little Rock, Arkansas: August House, Inc., 1995.

May, Antoinette. *Haunted Houses of California.* San Carlos, California: Wide World Publishing, 1990, 1993.

Munn, Debra D. *Ghosts on the Range.* Boulder, Colorado: Pruett Publishing Company, 1989.

Murray, Earl. *Ghosts of the Old West.* Chicago, Illinois: Contemporary Books, Inc., 1988.

Myers, Arthur. *A Ghosthunter's Guide.* Chicago, Illinois: Contemporary Books, Inc., 1993.

Smith, Barbara. *Ghost Stories of the Rocky Mountains.* Renton, Washington: Lone Pine Publishing, 1999.

Sutton, John G. *Do You Believe in Ghosts?* Boston, Massachusetts: Element Children's Books, 1999.

Time-Life Books, Inc. *Mysteries of the Unknown.* Richmond, Virginia: Time-Life Books, Inc., 1988.

Young, Richard and Judy Dockey. *Ghost Stories from the American Southwest.* Little Rock, Arkansas: August House, Inc., 1991.

Photo Credits:

Alabama—The Humming Bird, passenger train of the Louisville and Nashville
        Railroad, rolls through Birmingham, Alabama. ©1954 L & N Collection,
        University of Louisville Archives

California—Aerial view of the Winchester Mystery House. © Winchester Mystery House

Delaware—The Woodburn Mansion. © D. Michels

Georgia—Statue of Savannah's Waving Girl. © Savannah Convention and Visitors
        Bureau

Kentucky—The Historic, or Natural, Entrance is perhaps the best known sight in the
        Mammoth Cave National Park. / Broadway, or Main Cave, is a colossal
        underground canyon at the park. © National Park Service

Massachusetts—The Salem Witch Museum building in Salem, Massachusetts. ©
        Salem Witch Museum

New York—Margaretta Fox (left), Catharine Fox (middle), and a woman named Mrs.
        Fish (right). This photo was originally titled: Mrs. Fish and the Misses Fox:
        The Original Mediums of the Mysterious Noises at Rochester Western, NY.
        (1852 Currier lithograph of the Fox Sisters from the Department of Rare
        Books and Special Collections, University of Rochester)

Oregon—Heceta Head Lighthouse. © Don W. Ford

Tennessee—Roadside historic marker. © Yolanda G. Reid

Washington—Main entrance to Seattle's Pike Place Market. © George D. Hallowell

West Virginia—Circa 1882-1886 photo of John Brown's Fort. The building to the
        right of the fort was the former Armory superintendent's office.
        Advertisements painted on buildings and walls were aimed at rail
        travelers passing through Harpers Ferry. © Harpers Ferry National
        Historical Park

How to Find Lost Treasure in All Fifty States
and Canada, too!

Also by Joan Holub

Introduction

Is there a lost treasure where you live?

Yes! There are lost treasures in every state in the United States and all over the world. Treasures can be hidden underground, in swamps, oceans, caves, houses, and even backyards. Lost treasures could be just about anywhere!

How does treasure get lost?

Nobody loses a treasure on purpose. So how do so many get lost?

Before there were banks, some people kept their money and jewels safe by burying them. Miners often hid their gold and silver underground or in caves while they dug for more. They all wanted their hiding places to be secret. Sometimes they didn't tell anyone where it was—not even their families. When they died, no one knew where their treasures were hidden.

Pirates who robbed ships could not put their stolen booty in a bank. Neither could outlaws who robbed banks, trains, or stagecoaches. They sometimes hid it. Often they died or went to jail before they could go back for their treasure.

Have you ever hidden something and then forgotten where it was? Imagine if you buried a treasure but couldn't find it when you went back to look. This has really happened!

The stories surrounding lost treasures are mysterious. Not everyone agrees on the facts of how some treasures were lost, who they belong to, what the treasures are worth, or even if all stories of lost treasure are true. Many treasure hunters believe the treasures in this book are real. But they don't know exactly where or how to find them. Will you be the one to figure out where a treasure is hidden?

Illinois
Cave In Rock Treasure

The treasure: Pirate loot and other treasures
Where it is: Along the west bank of the Ohio River in southeastern Illinois

In 1798, land west of the Ohio River was still largely ungoverned and unsettled by pioneers. Gangs of river pirates regularly robbed flatboat travelers and commercial boats traveling on the Ohio River.

A notorious limestone cave in a cliff on the west bank of the Ohio River was once a hideout for these river pirates. This cave, known as Cave In Rock, was a perfect lookout point. It was a huge, vaulted cavern that gave pirates an excellent view up and down the river. This made it easy to watch for unsuspecting travelers who the pirates could rob.

When Abraham Lincoln was just nineteen, his flatboat loaded with farm produce was attacked by pirates on the Ohio River. He was lucky. He escaped with minor injuries. The heartless river pirates sometimes murdered those they robbed and weighted their bodies so that they would sink to the bottom of the river. Often no one ever found out what had happened to the missing travelers.

One of these river pirates, a man named Wilson, opened a shabby tavern at Cave In Rock. He advertised liquor and entertainment. But unlucky river travelers who stopped at Wilson's cave were often robbed and killed.

Brothers Wiley and Micajah Harpe were two of the worst outlaws ever to hide out at Cave In Rock. The bloodthirsty Harpe brothers were so horrible that even the other pirates couldn't stand their evil ways. They once killed a man just for snoring too loudly. After the Harpe brothers pushed a man and his horse over a cliff for fun, the other out-laws had finally had enough. They banished the Harpes from Cave In Rock.

Pirates James Ford and Billy Potts often attacked ferry travelers on the Ohio River near Cave In Rock. It is believed that river pirates named Sam Mason, John Murrell, and Jack Sturdevant also used the cave as a base.

With so much robbing taking place along the Ohio River, many treasure hunters believe a lot of treasure lies buried in the area near Cave In Rock.

Today, Cave In Rock is part of an Illinois state park.